SHADOW LINE

Shadow Alliance Series

SHAWNA COLEING

Chapter 1

THE SLIVER of moon offered no illumination to the dark road as Liam pulled over to the shoulder, or what remained of the crumbly edge. Two wheels of his unregistered 1994 Ford Escort, which he'd bought that day for cash, remained on the pavement. Anyone coming down the long stretch of deserted road should have no trouble spotting him and hopefully would stop.

He paused after exiting the car, resting his arm on the top of the door and breathing in the unfamiliar country air. The buzz out here was more intense than that of the city where he spent most of his time. The high-pitched whir of crickets vibrated in his unaccustomed ears. But despite the strange calming effect it had on him, tonight wasn't about smelling roses.

After the short reprieve, he moved to the front of the car and lifted the hood, locking it into place before backing up several feet to stand in the beam of the headlights.

He crossed his arms, assessing the scene. Details

were an important part of any job. Sometimes he got away with mediocre work, but these guys weren't fools, and he couldn't afford to be careless.

He reached into his holster and drew out a pistol, firing into the radiator. Steam erupted from the engine with a satisfying hiss. This was soon followed by the rumble of an engine in the distance that made a muscle in Liam's jaw flinch.

They were early.

He guessed there would be three men at a minimum. All armed.

After tugging his cap low on his forehead, he anchored his arms on the side of the engine bay, leaning far enough under the hood to look like he had no idea what he was doing.

The headlights of the approaching vehicle created living shadows of the nearby trees, but when the light fully engulfed Liam and his car, it became clear that the truck wasn't slowing. He moved into the middle of the road, waving his arms like any stranded citizen would.

He waited until the truck was almost stopped before covering his face with his forearm as though protecting his eyes from the lights.

He had to move fast. He was a sitting duck out in front like he was, and it wouldn't take these guys long to figure out something was wrong.

Jogging to the driver's side, he kept his head low.

"Hey," he called out when he reached the window. "Thanks for stopping."

The driver rolled down the window. He had heavy eyebrows that kept his eyes in shadow. He growled down to Liam, "We're in a hurry. Can't help you out. You'll have to move out of the way and wait for someone else."

Liam took note of the two men in the cab. Neither one of them was familiar to him, but he still tapped down on his cap to make sure it hid his face. He didn't want to kill anyone tonight if he didn't have to, and he couldn't risk being identified.

"Ah, come on. I've already been out here for hours."

"Hours, huh?" The driver shifted. A move that Liam recognized. "Then why is your engine still steaming?"

Nope, these guys weren't stupid. Liam had his gun out and fired before the men in the cabin could react. He hated when things didn't go as planned.

After the two men were taken care of, he moved back several steps, keeping his gun raised, waiting for a further onslaught from the back of the truck. When things stayed quiet, he circled around, listening above the din of the surrounding insects for movement. But all was quiet. Only two guys on this load. It wasn't often he got a break. That would simplify things somewhat.

He went back to the cabin of the truck and wrenched open the driver's door, pulling out the two dead men and throwing them down the embankment. Then he wiped down the blood before going to inspect the cargo.

If his intel was good, and it usually was, he already knew what waited for him in the back, but it still twisted his guts in knots. He might be on the wrong side of the law himself, but what these guys were doing crossed a line that should never be crossed, even in a messed-up world. Laws existed that were universally understood as what gave man his humanity.

He could have left it for the police to confirm, but he needed to see the cargo for himself. To remind himself how far a person can fall if they weren't careful.

Pulling open the back, he didn't notice the shadow inside in time, and he was met with the bottom of a boot impacting his head, leaving him flat on his back with his head fuzzy and spinning.

Ignoring his split lip, his only option now was to react or die. He forced his body to roll sideways. A bullet grazed his arm, but he gained enough focus to jump to his feet and dive tackle his assailant to the ground.

The gun went skidding and the two men wrestled off the pavement. The other man punched him in the side and got an arm around his throat. Liam threw an elbow back, knocking the wind out of his assailant and loosening his grip so Liam could rip out of his grasp and get on his feet. He reached for his weapon but found it missing.

When his foe joined him upright, Liam executed a roundhouse kick to his face that sent him over the embankment and into the darkness below.

Liam scrambled to find his gun, then held it steady while he listened for the man. He tipped his head sideways to hear through the hum of crickets, but there was no movement below and it was too dangerous and unnecessary to go after the guy. If he was still conscious, it would take him time to scramble up the hill, and by then, Liam would be gone.

He secured his gun and returned to the truck,

pulling himself up into the back. He winced at the pain in his right arm. It would probably need stitches, but he didn't have time for that. Instead, he pulled his gun out again and took a breath. He didn't expect there to be any more guys on the other side of the internal door, but he also couldn't be sure of the reaction from the payload inside.

He pushed up the latch on a container that filled most of the back of the truck and braced himself as gasps echoed in the small space. The sound confirmed that his intel was correct, but he wanted to make sure all the women where accounted for in this shipment. He could do nothing for any that might be missing, but he wanted to know. Using a small penlight, he counted eight young women huddled inside. His tension eased. They were all there. Some of them appeared to be drugged, and others recoiled in terror. One woman looked angry and had a cut on her cheek that appeared fresh. She was lucky to be alive. These guys rarely put up with trouble. They simply removed it.

He kept his gun at his side so he wouldn't frighten them, but he wouldn't put it away. Not yet. "If you can speak English, I want you to know that you're safe now. I'm taking you to local police, who will get you home."

The angry woman moved, and Liam gripped his gun more securely. Not that he could blame her if she wanted to attack. He shined the light in her face to dissuade her from doing something they'd both regret. "Those men can't hurt you anymore. I'm going to get you home to your families." Still nothing. "Miss, do you speak English?" he said to the angry one.

"Yes."

"We're in the middle of nowhere, and there is nowhere else for you to go besides staying where you are. The only way I can get you to safety is to keep you where you are. Can I trust you to look after the others and explain what's happening?"

"You'll shut the door again?"

"I have to. I'm sorry." He hated that it was necessary to lock them inside again. "It's for your safety this time instead of your captivity."

"But we have no choice?" Her eyes dipped to his gun.

"No."

"Then don't tell me we are not still captive."

"It won't be long." He shut the door before his guilt led him to explain himself. He'd taken a big risk to save them and felt worse than he thought he should. But he couldn't demand trust from these women. They had every right to be suspicious of everyone.

Before leaving the site, Liam ran his car off the side of the road, then headed for the nearest town. If the police found the scene he left behind, it wouldn't matter. The car couldn't be traced back to him, and the men were most likely known felons. The mysterious event that took place on this deserted road would be filed away as a rival's ambush. Not completely void of truth.

Liam drove carefully, but it wasn't until he was back on the highway that he was able to avoid potholes. Each bump jarred him as if he were sardined in the back of the truck with the others. He'd never admit it, but he was glad he wouldn't have to face the women again. He might not be the one who locked them in the back originally, but he felt responsible for the man who did.

Pulling up in front of the police station was a welcome relief, and once he turned off the engine, he didn't waste time hanging around. He'd used gloves, so there was no need to wipe down his prints, and he'd been careful about wrapping his bleeding arm so it wouldn't leave DNA traces.

The police didn't have his name on record, but they might have his DNA in connection to other criminal activities that would send him to prison if he was caught. No matter how good a deed he just did, he didn't delude himself into thinking he saved these girls because he was a good person. He'd made peace a long time ago with the fact that he was a villain.

He could see the movement of officers inside. His mouth twitched as he honked the horn with several long blasts, then jumped from the truck and sprinted off into the safety of the shadows.

Chapter 2

EMILY SPRINTED UP THE HILL. Her lungs burned in response to the cold air she sucked in. But she preferred the scream of her lungs over the scream-filled nightmare she'd woken from that morning. She didn't get them often these days, but no matter what she did or how hard she prayed, running was the only way she'd found that gave her any relief. Exchange one pain for another.

Ignoring the searing in her chest, she focused on the large eggshell-blue house at the top of the hill. She couldn't see the peeling paint or the rotting steps, and it wasn't obvious from that distance that it was abandoned, but none of that dissuaded her from considering that house to be her favorite and the destination of her run.

When the hill flattened out, she tucked her head down for one last hard push. The sounds around her flattened as she focused on the road and the slap of her feet hitting the pavement. Her steps beat in a rhythm against her heavy breathing.

At the edge of the driveway, she slowed to a stop,

propping her hands onto her knees and slowing her breathing. She swallowed hard against the thickness in her throat that came with the exertion and looked up the driveway to the house.

After shaking out her jelly legs, she trudged forward and climbed up to the large porch, skipping the top step with the last vestiges of her energy. Then she slid down against a balustrade, tucking her legs through the railing and dangling her feet off the edge.

With her ankles crossed, her heel bounced off the side of the porch while the chilly April air cooled the sweat that dripped from her temple. She could always count on a breeze up here, even on the stillest days. Perfect for the hot summer days that lie ahead.

Her gaze drifted across the landscape that couldn't be adequately admired without a full sweep of the surroundings. It didn't matter how many times she came up here, the view always lifted her spirits. Today especially. Under the cloudy sky, the lake was a fuzzy mirror of the newly sprouting trees that blanketed the hill on the far side of the water.

She'd always adored this house, even as a little girl, when it wasn't the view that captured her as much as the house itself, sitting in its regal position at the top of the hill. The old farmhouse had a large wraparound deck and an abundance of windows, from the wide bays on the first floor to the arched alcoves that would have brought light to the attic.

It was a mystery back then, owned by a family with older children she had no connection to. As a girl, she would often daydream about what it would be like to have that home, compared to the one-story Cape Cod she lived in.

These days she didn't mind the one-bedroom retreat she'd created for herself above her parent's garage. At twenty-seven years old, living with her dad was not ideal, but after returning from the city, it was as far as her fear would allow her to escape. If she had owned this house, however, things might have been different, and there was a time when she thought it could happen.

A man named Richard Hargrave had bought the house not long after she had returned from living in New York City.

He wasn't someone she would have expected to become friends with. But she had a lot in common with an old man who looked like he fought a losing battle to carry the weight of the world on his shoulders. The sadness that life bestowed upon him spoke to the fear and dread she carried around inside herself and hinted that maybe his wounds were greater than hers.

His presence in Oakridge meant she was no longer the most broken person in that small town. But when Richard had admired a piece of furniture she'd created, that small conversation blossomed into a tentative friendship that felt a bit like family before he passed away. He never shared much about his past, but neither did she. And she knew they both carried a lot of regrets.

She grieved for him, but couldn't help her hope that he'd left the house to her. That aging residence, along with the man who owned it, felt like it understood her better than most.

After he died, and she found out he'd left it to his

estranged son, she continued to use it as a refuge when the son never turned up to claim it. He must have been paying the taxes because she watched and waited for a foreclosure that never came.

Rumors of the unknown son centered on a general agreement that he lived as a monk in Italy somewhere. But small-town gossip was unreliable. She knew from personal experience when new theories arose regularly to explain why she had returned from the city. They never came close to what really happened. But she preferred the rumors over the truth.

But Richard hadn't left her empty-handed. She reached into her shirt and pulled out the pendant he'd given to her before he died. It was beautiful and even though he told her it wasn't worth much, she knew it was more valuable than he let on. She suspected the diamonds were real, but it didn't matter because she'd never part with it. It was a reminder that she didn't want to finish life carrying regret like Richard had.

A fresh wind rushed across the yard and sent a chill close to the bone. A shiver sent her shoulders up to her ears and she pressed her hands to the side of her face to stem the ache creeping into her head. It was time to go home.

Liam stretched out on his couch, enjoying the thought that by now the police would have found the girls and removed them from their prison. Knowing they were safe from harm eased the weight he was doomed to carry for life. He grabbed a baseball sitting on the table at the head of the couch and threw it toward the ceiling, catching it just before it smashed into his nose. He held it there for a moment, waiting for the sweep of exhaustion he had hoped would catch up to him eventually, but it remained elusive.

He tossed the ball a few more times, but when his brain refused to succumb, he got up and poured himself a stiff drink, knocking it back in one quick gulp. The burn should have been a familiar comfort, but he didn't hide the wince as he held the empty glass down by his leg, tapping a finger on it while he surveyed his apartment. It was filled with nice things that he'd acquired both legally and otherwise. But even with nicer views than most people had in the city, he still felt like a bird trapped in a cage. Lifestyle, no matter how elegant, did little to soothe a troubled soul, and his surroundings only served to remind him that the money that afforded him these luxuries was ill-gotten gain that someone else had to pay the price for.

His cell phone rang, and he almost ignored it. But when he walked over to glance at the name, he decided to answer. It was an odd hour for his friend to be calling. He didn't lift the phone, just swiped his finger across the screen and put it on speaker.

"Marcus, what can I do for you?"

"Liam." He sounded out of breath. "I don't know what you did, but Kyle's coming for you."

Liam snatched up the phone. "What? Why?"

'Why' wasn't really the question Liam needed answering. He knew exactly *why*, but a perpetually guilty conscience meant he took on a practiced innocent position out of habit. What he really needed to know from Marcus was how Kyle knew.

"I don't know, but if you're at home you need to leave, now."

The line went dead.

Marcus had earned a certain amount of trust from Liam, and he wasn't the type of man prone to exaggeration, so Liam grabbed his jacket and his keys, making a U-turn when he reached the door. Kyle moved quickly when he was motivated so Liam headed for the window instead.

He leaned out to the fire escape to scan the alley below. It was empty, but that could change in an instant.

After climbing out onto the landing, he closed the window, then jumped over the railing, sliding down the ladder rather than wasting time with the steps.

When he reached the street, he ran for the corner, twisting around discreetly to check the road at the front of his building. He spotted three men exiting a van that was parked right behind his car.

He tucked his keys into his pocket and ran back up the alley, climbing over the fence to make his escape on a back street.

After running flat out for a mile to get well clear of his building, he turned left, continuing at a comfortable jog for several more miles.

A couple blocks from his destination, he entered a 7-Eleven and bought two giant slices of pepperoni pizza, then walked the rest of the way.

A Rottweiler raced toward him as soon as he

grabbed hold of the chain-link fence. He tossed one slice of pizza over the top to shut him up, then scaled quickly and dropped to the ground and gave the dog a pat before feeding him the other slice.

"It's just me, Killa. No need to get all wound up." The dog wagged his stub of a tail and followed Liam toward the side door of a garage with a large sign that read "Marty's Automotive."

The run-down look of the outside did not accurately reflect the interior, or the man who owned the place, but the security on the door did.

Liam punched in the code for the lock that he only knew because he'd looked over Marty's shoulder one morning. The man trusted Liam more than he should have.

When the red light changed to green, Liam told Killa to sit and stay, then he went inside, closing the door quietly behind him and turning on the lights.

The buzzing flick of the fluorescence rattled the still air as he headed for the back of the room where a black 1946 Indian Chief motorcycle sat in all its glory. Every time he looked at her, it took his breath away.

He took a moment to admire the view before he grabbed the handlebars and yanked it up off the kickstand, until the metallic clank of a cocking shotgun echoed through the room and he froze. His fingers loosened off the bike, and he lifted his hands.

The heavy steps of the newcomer thumped across the greasy concrete floor as Liam turned slowly, his hands lifted high.

The man had the gun anchored against his shoulder, ready to fire. "What do you think you're doing?"

Liam shrugged. "Sorry. Something came up that couldn't wait till morning."

"What'd you do to my dog?"

Liam snorted. "I can't help it if he enjoys taking a bite out of pizza more than out of me."

The man lowered his gun a fraction. "You're gonna make him fat."

"Marty, he is a good dog who deserves to be spoiled now and then."

The namesake of the business was a solidly built man in his fifties. He was a good mechanic, but what most people didn't know was that his real skill was in restoration.

Marty lowered the gun all the way. "Fine, but how'd you get in here? It looks like my whole security ensemble has failed me."

"Change your code for the door and you'll be fine. As for Killa, if I were anyone else, I'd be a dead man."

"We'll see. What are you doing here in the middle of the night anyway? You scared me half to death."

"You didn't look real scared behind that barrel."

"I could have shot you, you know. Why didn't you come get me?"

"I didn't want to wake you, and I need my bike."

"I'm not done with her yet."

"Is she roadworthy?"

"Are you kidding? 'Course she is. But bringing her back into her full glory is a delicate process that takes time."

"I realize that, but it's an emergency."

"Well, she's your bike. You gonna bring her back in one piece?"

"You know how I feel about this bike. I'll protect her with my life."

"Okay then, I'll get the door."

While Marty went to the front of the garage, Liam rolled the bike around. The Indian was one thing he owned fair and square. The only lie in that card game was his poker face, but the straight flush that won him the hand — and the bike — was real.

"Where you headed?" Marty asked before Liam started the bike.

"Good question." Unfortunately, Kyle knew a lot of Liam's local associates. He probably even knew about Marty. "If anyone comes asking about me, you tell them you haven't seen me since last week."

"That bad, huh?"

"Could be worse."

"Could it?"

"I could already be dead."

"You need a place to hide out?"

"No, I've got a place outside the city where I can lie low for a day or two. After that, I'll come up with a plan."

"Well, good luck to ya."

"Thanks, Marty."

As Liam headed for the highway, his thoughts became more and more conflicted. Peter Black was the last person he wanted to see right now. Last time they had spoken was a couple years ago when Peter had called in a favor for a friend of his, a guy named Oliver, if Liam remembered correctly. He'd never found out how things had turned out, choosing instead to escape the shadow of a man who made him feel both welcome and guilty at the same time. If he was lucky, he wouldn't have to even set eyes on the man. Peter's property was big enough that if he laid low, Peter would never know he was there.

Chapter 3

PETER SAT up straight in bed, his heart racing. When his wife mumbled beside him, he slid his hand across the sheet and rubbed her arm before she rolled over.

He couldn't remember having a bad dream, but the way his muscles were tensed, he must have.

He lumbered down the steps to the kitchen for a glass of water that always helped to shrug off any anxiety that turned up in the night, but after filling his glass and wandering around downstairs for several minutes, his nerves weren't settling.

After depositing his empty cup in the sink, he continued his roaming in the living room in a half-hearted attempt to silence the urging that compelled him to stay. But this feeling was not unfamiliar territory. He knew the tension squeezing at his heart couldn't be attributed to any nightmare, and he groaned, scrubbing his hands over his face as the reality of what he was now dealing with settled in.

It had been several days since he'd slept well

through the night. He expected tonight to be his chance to catch up, but he knew that call too well to ignore.

He finally surrendered his desire to go back to sleep and instead dropped onto the couch in the dark, resting his head in his hands.

He'd sit and wait for a few minutes, but if God stayed quiet, he was going back to bed.

As he waited, his thoughts remained silent, his muscles twitched in anticipation. He wasn't supposed to sit.

"So I can't go back to bed, and I can't sit down." He looked down at the floor. *Kneeling perhaps?* No, that wasn't it either.

With no idea where to go or what to do, Peter did the only thing he could. He paced the room and prayed whatever popped into his mind.

He prayed for peace and safety for his family and friends. He thought of Oliver and Morgan in New York City and smiled. They were a force to be reckoned with. The work they did these days saved a lot of lives. He prayed for their wisdom.

On his third pass across the living room, he caught sight of the edge of the barn out the big picture window. He stepped closer to get a better look at it, then moved on in his route around the room.

"Give Jemi encouraging words to pass on to those whose lives she touches."

His eyes focused on the barn again as he passed. This time he didn't pause but kept going, thanking God for everything he could think of. But when he saw the barn a third time, he had to stop and admit that it stirred something in the pit of his stomach.

"Are you kidding me?" He looked at the clock on the wall. It was after three in the morning. He knew his night was over, but he refused to budge for a moment. God had asked him to do some strange things over the years, but it was the inconvenient ones that irked him the most. He preferred the risky ones.

He put his hands on his hips in one last stand, but he knew it was a waste of time. In the end, he always gave in to what God asked. Whether or not it turned out to be something significant, obedience was always important.

"There's a terrorist in my barn, right?" He shook his head and went to get his coat.

He stood on the porch in the dark, watching the barn for any sign of movement. It was most likely a waste of time to be cautious, but if he was going to do this, he'd do it his way, like he was on one of his missions. It might make him look like a fool, but who was looking?

He crept across the lawn, sticking to the darkest parts of the yard. His thoughts drifted back to the time he met his wife in that dark compound in Iraq. He could have made a number of different choices that would have meant she'd be dead now. Possibly him as well. His stomach tightened at the thought of losing her. She was everything he never knew he wanted, and she added a richness to his life that he wouldn't have asked God for because he didn't know it existed.

Pushing aside a longing for his wife, who was asleep

warm in bed while he stalked through his own yard like a lunatic, he moved to the side of the barn, heading for the door he knew would be unlocked.

His fingers wrapped around the cold metal knob and turned slowly. The door would squeak at halfway open, so he only opened it far enough to slip through.

A ladder leaning against the wall was enough cover to start with. He crouched behind it and waited, listening. But everything was silent.

God, you better not be messing with me.

He moved from his hiding spot and traversed the barn, stopping at the midpoint and listening again. That's when he caught a thread of sound from behind and his body reacted from years of training.

Throwing his elbow backward, he smashed into a wall that grunted, then he twisted and swung his arm around the intruder's neck, slipping behind him and dropping him to the ground. His foe was well trained, too, and quickly reversed their positions, but Peter was ready. He loved that barn and knew the layout and where every tool was located. He lifted his knee, moving the other man's weight so he could reach out above his head and grab the shovel that he kept there. His fingertips only grazed the handle, so he kicked his legs out, not only catching his opponent but also giving him enough push to grab the handle of the shovel, bringing it immediately around on the intruder, who spun around to protect his head and took the hit on his shoulder. Peter jumped on him then, grabbing an arm and wrenching it around to incapacitate the man.

"I'll break it if I have to," Peter said, twisting to the point where he knew he was close.

"Black," the man cried out in pain. "Peter."

"Identify yourself," Peter commanded.

"Liam. Liam Hargrave."

Peter lessened his grip, but only marginally. "Liam?"

"Yeah." The word came out strained from his effort to keep his arm intact. "You mind?"

Peter let go but had the shovel ready. "Is that really you?"

"You know anyone who would want to pretend they're me?"

"Fair point," Peter said, depositing the shovel back against the wall. "What are you doing here? And why are you sneaking around my barn? I could have really hurt you."

Liam stretched his shoulder and squeezed at the pain. "No kidding. Man, you still got it. Although, that wasn't really a fair fight. I knew it was you and didn't want to hurt you."

"Then why didn't you say something? Why not come to the house?"

"Sorry, I didn't want to intrude. And I was just trying to sneak past you. All I need is a place to crash. I had hoped I'd be here and gone without you knowing."

"Why? You know you're welcome in my house any time."

"It's been almost two years, Peter."

"And your point? You know my door is always open."

"Yeah, well. I've been busy."

"You've been a ghost is what you've been. I looked for you. Wanted to thank you for the work you did in New York."

"Maybe I didn't want to be found. So it worked out?"

"It did."

"Good."

"But that doesn't explain why you're in my barn in the middle of the night and not in my house."

"It's not that complicated."

"Then enlighten me."

"Because I knew you'd want to get involved."

"And that's a bad thing?"

"I don't need you involved."

"So you're in trouble, then?"

"What is this, twenty questions? I just needed to get out of town for a bit."

"The police looking for you? FBI?"

"Everybody's always looking for me. But no, it's not the police I'm evading."

Peter headed for the door. "Fine, you don't have to explain, but at least come inside. It'll be light soon. I'll make you a cup of coffee. I take it you haven't slept all night?"

"No."

"I guess there's no point in either of us trying to get any sleep. You can stay as long as you like, but don't leave without saying goodbye. Jemi would be furious."

. . .

When they came into the dim light of the house, Peter noticed the blood dripping down Liam's face. "Looks like I got you good."

Liam lifted his hand and pressed a finger against the cut. "Only 'cause I didn't want to hurt you."

"Whatever you need to tell yourself," Peter said as he grabbed the first aid kit from the cupboard and tossed it to Liam. "You remember where the bathroom is?"

"Yeah."

"Great, you clean up and I'll get us coffee."

Peter looked in the general direction of the bathroom while he waited for the coffee to percolate. Liam was the last person he'd expected to run across tonight, but he must be in serious trouble if he was trying to hide out unnoticed in the barn. If it had been anybody else, Peter would have pushed for more information, but with Liam, it was complicated. He had learned way back when he trained Liam that the man needed to find his own way into things. Peter knew if he pressed, Liam would shut down. Even get angry.

Liam wasn't the type of person who liked help. It took Peter a long time to get Liam to trust him but it still felt like Liam was waiting to be double-crossed. He was a strong and capable man, but with issues of the heart, he reacted like a cornered animal.

Years ago Peter had been patient enough to get behind Liam's wall, but those walls had long since been repaired and stood in the way of Peter being of any use.

It would take something very drastic to get through again.

When the two men sat down at the kitchen table, Peter waited for Liam to make the first move. He hated long gaping silences, so Peter kept his mouth shut.

After several minutes, Liam finally said, "So you're not going to do that thing you do?"

"What thing do I do?"

"That thing where you seem to know more about me than I do?"

"I guess that's up to you. I'm quite happy to sit here and enjoy the serenity of the early morning."

"Liar."

Peter shrugged, then took a sip of coffee, smiling into his cup.

Liam rapped his knuckles on the table. "Anything's better than your silent contemplation of the situation. Why don't you give it a whirl?"

"Only because you insist." Peter waited for the annoyed crease between Liam's eyes to settle before he continued. "Well, you've obviously done something you shouldn't have."

"Did God tell you that?"

Peter chuckled, refusing to take the bait. He knew Liam was much more wary of God's interaction in his life than he let on. "No, I worked that one out on my own."

"Well, you're only half right."

"Which half?"

"I did something I should have, but there are those who don't agree."

"Sounds like an excuse."

"It's not. So that's the best you've got? No deep wisdom of the ages for me?"

"Nothing springs to mind." Peter could see the disappointment in the downturn of his friend's lips. Liam was a contradiction. He had always been curious about God, but afraid too. Afraid and hopeful that he'd hear the words he was longing to hear. But unsure if the effect of those words would be good or bad.

God, you're going to have to give me something here. I've got nothing. "Can I ask what you did?"

"Got some people out of trouble who didn't deserve it."

"So you're a hero."

"Is that supposed to be a joke?"

"Is it a joke to you? The idea that you're the good guy for once?"

Liam leaned back with a smirk on his face. "That's more like it."

"I'm glad you're amused."

"I can't have a visit with my old friend Peter without getting a good pep talk straight from the creator of the universe himself."

"God didn't tell me that either."

"No?"

"No. I just know you too well."

"Oh really."

"Yeah. Just like your cocky arrogance tells me I've hit a nerve."

Liam took a sip of coffee and stared into the cup. "I guess I'm an open book. But so are you. When are you going to hit me with the real heavy God stuff? I know you're dying to."

"Yeah?"

Liam grinned into his coffee. "It's your modus operandi."

Peter sent up a quick prayer before he said, "You're here for a reason."

"Yeah, I am. You had a barn, and I needed a place to hide out."

"I'm sure you know of a lot of places you could have gone."

"If only. Trust me. If I could have gone anywhere else, I would have. All I needed was a good place to hide."

"If that's all it is, then why did God wake me up in the middle of the night and send me out to find you? There's nowhere you can hide from him."

That wiped the smile off Liam's face. "I didn't come here to be preached at."

"You're the one who asked, remember?"

"You always did treat me like a kid."

"That's because there's a scared little kid inside of there who needs to find some healing. You need to let him out." Peter knew he'd crossed a line even as the words were coming out of his mouth. Liam pushed because he wanted Peter to say something he could react against. He needed something to push away from. And Peter had given it to him.

Liam's mouth was set in a hard line. "Thanks for the

coffee." He stood up from the table as Peter's wife entered the room. She had uncanny timing.

"Liam? My word, what are you doing here? I thought I heard more than one voice."

"Sorry, Jemi, I was just leaving." He leaned in to give her a kiss on the cheek.

"Nonsense, you can't leave yet. You need breakfast. Come into the kitchen and keep me company while I make it."

"I'd love to, but I can't."

Jemi blocked his escape. "You're telling me, if you stay and have breakfast, you will die?"

"No."

"Will the world end?"

"No."

"Then stop making excuses." She grabbed his hand and pulled him with her.

Peter watched as they headed for the kitchen. Jemi had a gift that Peter had always admired. Her stepping in and taking care of Liam had little to do with nurturing and more to do with recognizing what needed to be done. It constantly amazed Peter how God used the two of them as a team. They never planned it. It was just how it worked. God done it from the first time they met. Peter thought he was saving her, but they ended up saving each other.

Whether or not he'd messed up with Liam, God could still do what he needed to do. He didn't need Peter to be perfect.

As he ran a hand across his forehead, he wiped away grit he didn't know was there. He looked at his dirty fingers, then down at his clothes. They were filthy and bloodstained and Jemi hadn't even batted an eyelid when she saw him. She'd seen enough in her life to remain unfazed by something as insignificant as blood and dirt.

When Peter returned to the kitchen, he was greeted by riotous laughter.

Jemi wiped a stray tear from her eye as she caught her breath. "Has Liam ever told you the story about the time he dressed up like Elvis to get backstage at a casino?"

"Yes, I'm pretty sure I've heard that one before."

Jemi sighed. "Liam, I forgot what a good storyteller you were. You should come around more often. I need to laugh more."

Liam's phone rang. He saw Marcus' name. "Sorry, I need to take this."

Jemi caught Peter's eye when Liam turned around and walked out of the room to answer it. She lifted her eyebrows and Peter moved closer. "He's trying to escape." She served up a couple of eggs on a plate and slid them across the counter.

"Yeah, he said someone was after him."

"No, I mean, the life he's in. Whatever he's done that has people after him, he sees it as penance, but never really feels forgiven for the life he's led. It's never going to be enough. It's got his claws into him, but it's not what he wants."

"Did he tell you that?" Peter said, taking a bite.

"Not in so many words. I can just feel it. He's ashamed. He's looking for your approval."

Peter opened his mouth to respond, but Liam came back into the room.

"I've got some good news," he said, slipping his phone into his back pocket. "That was a friend of mine. He told me there was a misunderstanding. He thought things were worse than they were, so I can head back home."

"And you can trust this friend?" Peter asked.

"Yeah, Marcus hasn't steered me wrong yet."

"So, no one is after you?"

"Apparently not."

"Well, that's a relief."

"Thanks for the breakfast, Jemi. I'll get out of your hair."

"You sure you won't stay longer? It would be nice to catch up a bit more."

"Thank you, but I've got some business I need to take care of." Liam noticed the pain in Jemi's smile, and he dropped his eyes to the floor. "I'll visit again soon."

Jemi chose not to state what she knew to be true, that if he walked out that door, he had no intention of coming back. He was too used to running away. It was easier than staying and dealing with the problem. "I'm glad you're safe. If you ever feel unsafe, for any reason, you know where to find us."

"Thanks, Jemi. I know I can be hardheaded with you two, but I do consider you to be good friends, and I don't have many of those."

Peter walked him out. With each step, his concern

grew. He stopped Liam at the door. "You sure you don't want to hang around? It could be good for you, and I can promise not to mention God."

"Thank you, but I can't."

Peter tightened his jaw to keep his mouth shut. He wanted to beg Liam not to run away, but this time, he heeded the warning in his gut to be silent. "Okay, well, don't be a stranger. And next time you need a place to hide out, just knock. Please. I'm not a fan of assaulting people in my barn in the middle of the night. I'd rather get up and answer the door instead."

"I promise. I'll see ya."

"Yeah, see ya."

Liam slapped Peter on the arm and jogged down the front steps. Peter watched him until he disappeared from view but remained standing in the open door even when he heard the sound of the motorcycle fade away.

Jemi joined him, resting her hand on his shoulder. "He's not okay."

"No, I don't think he is."

"But we couldn't keep him here. We weren't supposed to. I didn't want to see him go, but I have the feeling he's about to run headlong into something. I just hope God can get through to him before it's too late."

Peter nodded. "So what now?"

"Right now, he needs a whole lot of prayer."

"That's exactly what I was thinking."

Chapter 4

"HELLO, and welcome to Maple Leaf. Is this your first time here?"

Patty's familiar Southern drawl came muffled through the office door. Her voice was louder and her words rolled a whole lot more than anything else you heard around here. Emily couldn't help but smile at the sharp contrast to the harsher upstate New York accent.

Peeking out of the window, she estimated the number of customers in line out to the parking lot. It wasn't an unfamiliar sight this time of the year, but it still astounded her how long people would wait for all-you-can-eat pancakes. Even if the maple syrup was made out the back. But she knew it wasn't just the food people came for. There was a coziness about the place, with its large fireplaces and timber rafters that drew people in and kept them there plate after plate.

When she had run back from New York City all those years ago with her tail between her legs, this was one of the few places she could relax. After growing up in a home that didn't feel like home, it was nice to have somewhere that felt welcoming.

"Before we're seated," came a woman's voice that sounded distinctly Manhattan, born and bread, "that table behind you — "

Emily cringed at the query she knew was coming from the woman. It didn't matter how many times Emily asked her dad to remove the table, he always refused, choosing instead to go on and on about how important it was to celebrate his daughter's gift for turning trees into something that people admired. He would finish off with, "I turn the sap into something wonderful and you do the same with the wood." The one time she'd persisted, he'd worked a guilt trip. "Where else can I put the pamphlets for nearby businesses? We need to support our own, you know. Do you have something against the other businesses in town?"

Listening to her dad was worse than enduring the occasion inquiry.

"This is handmade. I can tell." The woman's voice continued.

Emily would have to intervene. Patty could not be trusted to keep her mouth shut.

She moved quickly, slipping out of the office full of clutter and lodging herself between the table and the customer after a quick sidestep.

"Excuse me," she said once she was in position. "I couldn't help but overhear. You're admiring the table."

"Yes, it's absolutely exquisite. And I should know."

"Should you?" Emily didn't mean to sound rude, but she didn't want to open the wound.

"Oh yes. It's walnut." It was a statement, not a question.

"Yes, I believe it is," Emily said, shifting from one foot to the other in agitation.

"Can I ask where it was purchased?" the woman asked.

"It was a gift." Emily said this quickly to get the jump on Patty, who she could tell was eager to extol the virtues of the table and its maker.

"My goodness. That's wonderful. Are you able to point me in the direction of the artist?"

"I'm afraid not."

The woman's eyes shifted to Patty, then back again. "I think you would find that it is in the artist's best interest. I am looking for a signature piece for my home and can pay well."

"They don't do requests."

"I'd make it worth their while."

"No. They're, um, dead." Patty gasped behind Emily, who gritted her teeth.

"Oh my. That is unfortunate. I got a little excited there for a moment. This one isn't for sale by any chance?"

"No, I'm afraid not."

"Not for any price?"

"It belongs to the owner, who considers it to be priceless, so you're out of luck. I guess you'll just have to settle for the pancakes."

"That is unfortunate, but we did come firstly for your menu. You come very highly recommended. It's not the sort of place we usually eat, but we love to try new things. Especially while on vacation."

"Then I hope you enjoy your meal. Patty?" Emily turned to the waitress, whose perm looked like it had gone curlier since the morning. "You can show them to their table now."

Emily retreated to the office where she continued her decluttering, but the more she tidied the room, the more junk she found. Her dad had become a terrible hoarder since her mom had passed away. It was only recently that he began throwing stuff out for himself. A big step.

She was sifting through a drawer full of files from 1986 when a light tappity-tap-tap on the door broke her focus.

Emily didn't have to see who it was. She knew the knock. "Yes, Patty, what can I do for you?"

The waitress stuck her head through the door. "Day-ed?" She said the word *dead* in such a dramatic Southern accent, Emily almost couldn't understand what she had said.

"It was the only thing I could come up with so the woman would let it drop."

"But you lied."

"Yes, I did. I'm very sorry if I put you in an uncomfortable position."

"I just don't understand. That lady was rich. She would have paid you a lot of money to make her a table."

"Yes, she would have, but I wasn't lying when I told her the creator of the table doesn't do requests."

"But she's from the city."

"Yes, I realize."

"And isn't that why you went to the city all those years ago?"

"That was a long time ago."

"It wasn't that long." Patty sighed heavily and folded her arms across her ample bosom. "I can't figure you out, Emily Peterson."

"I can't figure me out either. But it doesn't matter. I came home because my dad needed me and with everything I need to do, I don't have time to make furniture."

"So the rumors aren't true, then?"

"Which ones? There are so many to choose from."

"I like to stick with the most simple explanations. I find those to be the most reliable."

"I didn't think any of them were simple."

"But you came back 'cause you were running away?" Her cheeks reddened. "I'm sorry. I shouldn't have said anything."

"I came back to help my dad. He was in a bad way after my mom died."

Patty squinted. "I don't think you give your dad enough credit."

"Don't you have tables to wait?"

"Oh!" Patty threw her arms up in the air and turned quickly, scooting out the door.

Emily tossed the files aside. The din of the restaurant had turned from a comfortable background noise to an irritation. She looked around the room, not satisfied but confident she'd made a dent. The rest of the work she had to do today could be done from home. Setting up social media posts for the week would be easier done on her own computer with the larger screen and there would be no more interruptions or distractions.

She scooted the chair over to the window and looked out again. This was the best time of year to increase their reviews and Facebook follows, which would help sales of other maple products, especially the leaf shaped candies and maple-scented candles, for the rest of the year. Early spring was a big season for the restaurant, but autumn's profits were driven by their online store.

Before she left, she detoured to the kitchen, where she knew she'd find her dad. The restaurant had all the kitchen staff they needed, but her dad was the original cook and liked to stay hands-on.

A cheer echoed down the hall, and from the volume, it sounded like it was made by the entire staff.

Emily pushed through the doors as the entire room erupted in one massive "Oooohhhh."

She watched her dad bend over to pick up a giant pancake from the floor.

He spotted his daughter as he straightened. "Forty-seven! That's a new flipping record." She crossed her arms and raised an eyebrow. "What? You're not impressed by your old man?"

"Dad, I'm glad you find amusement in the little things. That's all I'll say."

"Hey." One of the new busboys spoke up. "That is no small feat. I've tried it. It's not as easy as it looks."

"Okay, fine. Dad, you're amazing."

"Ah, that's sweet of you to say." He kissed her cheek as the kitchen went back to work.

"I'm just here to let you know I'm heading home. I'm going to work from there."

"Ha!" He turned back to his staff. "Robby, you owe me ten bucks."

The cook groaned and shoved his hand deep into his pocket, pulling out a wad of bills. He trudged over and stuffed them into his boss's hand, then he looked at Emily. "I thought you had more staying power."

"What?"

"I told him my office would defeat you. I tried to bet them all twenty bucks you'd give in before the end of the day, but no one would take the bet. Robby finally gave in at ten."

"You can give him his money back. It hasn't defeated me. I'm not done in there yet. I just have other important things to attend to."

Robby shook his head as he headed back to the stove. "Keep it. It'll save me giving it back later."

"I don't know why I put up with you guys," she mumbled playfully. "Have a nice day. I'll see you all tomorrow. And, Robby, when I'm done in there, you make sure to get your ten bucks back."

"Yeah, sure."

"Hang on," her dad said. "I'll walk you out."

Emily led the way, but when they got to her truck, he put a hand on her door to keep her from opening it. "You okay?"

"Of course I am. Why wouldn't I be?"

"Patty told me about the inquiry."

Emily lifted her eyes to the sky while she chose her words. This was an argument that no one would win.

"Dad, if you're worried about me, you could always move the table."

"And who would that help?"

"Me. It would help me. I have already explained to you that I'm done with all of that. I don't know why you feel the need to torture me with it." She wasn't sure if the hurt on his face was real or if he put it on to give her a hard time.

"I'm only trying to help. I don't think you should have given up so easily."

"I haven't given up. I still make stuff."

"That's not the same."

"I really don't want to have this conversation again. It's my decision to make, and I've made it. If you insist on keeping that piece where everyone can see it, then please don't chase me when I handle it my way."

"You know I only want what's best for you. I'm just worried that your mother — "

"She's got nothing to do with this."

"But you feel guilty."

"No, I don't. Not where she's concerned, anyway."

"But you gave it all away because of her. Or was it something else?"

Emily threw her arms in the air. "No, Dad. I didn't throw anything away. I told you I was ready to come home. It was time. I got everything out of New York I could. There was nothing else there I wanted."

"Then why are you always so sad?"

Her dad didn't bring up the past often, but it must simmer under the surface for him all the time. Emily wished she could help him let it go, but explaining the truth would make things much worse. "I've got to go."

"I worry about you."

"Well, don't. You've got me close by. You can keep an eye on me. Everything is fine."

She got into her truck and drove out without looking back. She knew he would stand there until she was out of view. She'd lied to her dad all these years about New York, but that didn't mean he believed her. Once, she had walked in on him mumbling about killing whoever had hurt his little girl. He wanted to help her face her demons not realizing that he probably wouldn't be able to handle it any better than she had.

When she pulled into her driveway, she stayed where she was, staring at the front door of the house she grew up in. As a girl, she couldn't wait to escape that place. Everything about it and her life there was a prison. There was only so much of her mother's manipulation that she could take. It didn't matter that her dad explained it away as mental health issues. She had controlled him as much as anyone, and it was because of her that he struggled with hoarding. He never held it against her. Never blamed her for his problems. But while he may have been able to forgive, Emily had trouble understanding what that even looked like. It was easier remembering her childhood as the source of all her problems. That way she could explain away why she was so helpless to get free of all the fear she had brought back with her from New York.

She got out of the truck and headed for the garage, intending to head straight up to her apartment and get to work, but after entering the downstairs, she made the mistake of running a finger over the newly sanded arm of a rocking chair she'd been working on for herself.

When she first returned from the city, she swore she would never create another thing, but it wasn't long before that vow became unbearable. Whenever she saw a piece of wood, it took shape and planted itself in her mind, provoking her until she brought it into existence. The first time she gave in, she discovered that the creative experience was cathartic, releasing her anxiety instead of heightening it as she had expected. It was the one thing that she could control, and giving those pieces away for free meant it couldn't control her.

She sat in the chair and pushed into a light rock. She rarely did pieces for herself, but with Richard's house remaining abandoned, she'd convinced herself that as the caretaker, she could make some small additions. And what that house needed more than anything was a rocking chair on the porch.

She rubbed her thumb over the edge of the arm. All that was left was the design she would etch into the wood there. But she had another project to finish first. Across the room sat two "in progress" bedside tables she was making for the sixtieth wedding anniversary of two friends she'd known for a lifetime.

Her Bible was sitting on one of them, but she couldn't remember leaving it there. Not that she was reliable about keeping track of it. If she read a scripture that dislodged painful memories, they acted like thorns attempting to escape their prison of skin. The discomfort was often more than she was brave enough to face and she'd drop her Bible anywhere in an attempt to escape.

At the memory of the last episode, her anxiety bubbled up and the images returned, sending her stomach tumbling. She swallowed back the bile, but she couldn't keep her mind from slipping back into that day. Then, the smell of blood filled the room around her, and she shot out of the chair, the back of the rocker bumping on the concrete floor.

Grabbing a piece of scrap sandpaper off her workbench, she dove for one of the bedside tables, shoving the Bible off so it tumbled to the floor. She scrubbed wildly at the top of the table, focusing on the wood dust that was accumulating on the surface until she felt safe enough to let in the world around her again.

When she sat back on her heals, she was shaking and her face was wet with tears she didn't realize she had been crying.

Nothing she did worked. No matter how hard she tried, she couldn't escape it. No matter how much scripture she repeated, how fast she ran, or how hard she scrubbed, she couldn't get free of it. Her past had branded her with a scar that even God couldn't do anything about. Somehow, she would have to make peace with the fact that she would live with this terror for the rest of her life. She gritted her teeth and kept sanding.

Chapter 5

LIAM PARKED his bike out in front of his apartment with a mixture of relief and disappointment. Part of him was glad to get away from Peter and Jemi, but he couldn't deny the pull he always had toward the pair. It's what had infuriated and intrigued him when he first met Peter. The sense of calm and peace about the man penetrated into Liam. It was that pull that had been the catalyst when he had crossed the line and connected with God many years ago.

But then he had been reminded of the world he actually lived in. Not the fairy tale that Peter lived in full of angels and demons and a God who loved you no matter what. Real life was hard and brutal, and if he didn't play by the rules of that kind of game, he'd be chewed up and spit out. As it was, he did a pretty good job of getting along in this world. He was very good at taking what he wanted. But if the world was about nothing more than survival of the fittest, why did his success leave him empty? And why did he feel the need to do good in order to assuage a guilt he shouldn't have?

When he had goaded Peter about the God stuff, some small part of him wanted to hear words that would explain it all and make everything right. He carried an impossible expectation that maybe God was the answer. It was a hope that wouldn't leave him alone, no matter how hard he tried to ignore it.

He pressed the heel of his hand across his eye to push back the tired that hung heavy on him. Maybe, when he fell into his bed today, he'd have the dreamless sleep he desperately needed.

After struggling to his door, he fumbled with the lock, his eyes half open, but it wasn't until he had crossed the threshold that he knew something was wrong. By then it was too late. A flash followed darkness as the world shut off around him.

Liam woke to find his arms tied to a chair. He squinted against a pounding headache until his eyes were able to focus and observe his surroundings. He recognized Marcus first, who sat on the couch. His left eye was swollen shut and his lip was split. He kept his eyes on his lap, staring at his hands, which were squeezed between his knees.

Three other men were in the room. One stood near the window holding a gun that hung at his side while he looked at his phone. Another, also armed, read the back of a book he had taken from the bookshelf.

"Oh good, you're awake," said a third man who was sitting in Liam's lounge chair, twisting a gold ring around his index finger. "Freddy was afraid he'd hit you too hard, weren't you, Freddy?" Freddy didn't respond. "I told him you were fine. You're tough enough to handle a bit of roughhousing. We used to give it to each other a bit, didn't we? Man. I don't know how many times I went home bleeding because of you. But it was all good, wholesome fun. Wasn't it?"

"Sure. Sorry I couldn't join you sooner." His words vibrated in his skull.

"It's only been twenty minutes. Now. Are you up to discussing business? Or do you need some time to recover? Can I get you a drink of water? Something stronger?"

Liam squeezed his eyes shut, trying to clear his head that was still fuzzy. "Sympathy is very unlike you, Kyle."

"Don't mistake my unceasing patience for sympathy. I have no reservations about killing you, no matter how good a friend you used to be."

"Used to? I'm hurt."

Kyle smirked. "You only have yourself to blame."

"How's that?"

"Among other things, there is that little business of you giving my shipment to the police."

"Among other things?"

"I've been keeping tabs on you."

"I'm flattered."

"Don't be. I haven't been able to pin you down until now."

"I don't know what you think I did, but I wouldn't

do something as stupid as handing a shipment of yours over to police."

"And yet you did. And I am really looking forward to finding out why. It's the reason I've tied you to a chair, after all."

"I'm sorry. I don't have any answers for you. It wasn't me."

"No? You weren't the one who threw Grazer down into the embankment and killed another two of my very competent men? Do you know how hard it is to find good help around here?"

"Grazer? I haven't seen Grazer in what — over a year? He does smoke a lot of pot. You sure he's not just paranoid?"

"He gave it up. Put on a bit of weight, too, so you can be excused for not recognizing him." Kyle leaned forward and lowered his voice. "But he knew you. You should have killed him like the others. But" — he stood and began pacing the room — "you live and you learn, right? I mean, you might not live, but I certainly have learned a lot about who I can trust."

Liam glanced over at Marcus, whose shoulders curved up against his ears like he was waiting to take a blow. Liam had learned a thing or two about who he could trust too. Maybe he should have listened to Peter and stayed put for a while. It wouldn't have mattered in the end. You can't run forever from a guy like Kyle. And that begged the question as to why Kyle hadn't killed him yet. The only thing that made sense was that he wasn't fully convinced of Liam's guilt. And with a guy like Grazer as the only witness, there was still hope.

"Kyle, I'm not sure what happened to your shipment, but I promise you, I had nothing to do with it."

"All right." Kyle put his hands on his hips and nodded at Freddy, who backhanded Liam. "If this is how you want to play this out."

Liam swallowed the blood in his mouth. He'd rather not have to replace the carpet if he lived through this.

"Let's start again, shall we? We are not in a courtroom. You are not innocent until proven guilty. I already know you're guilty, and it hurts me that you think you can play me like some easy mark. If I weren't the astute businessman I am, my emotions would have gotten the better of me and you'd already be dead. But I have more profitable ways of using you. You cost me a lot of money, and I want it back."

"You're probably better off killing me. I won't kidnap any girls for you."

Kyle laughed stiffly. "I wouldn't waste my time or yours on something like that. I learned a long time ago what a sorry excuse for a man you are. We both know you can't stomach it. However, I recall you boasting about a little trinket your dad got his hands on when we were a couple of ratbags running around on the streets together. You remember that?"

Liam ran his tongue along his split lip. "That was a story I made up to sound impressive. I had self-esteem issues back then."

Kyle nodded to Freddy, who walked over to Liam and punched him in the stomach.

While Liam recovered, Kyle perused the room and stopped, picking up a vase with plastic flowers. He pulled the flowers out and dropped them on the floor, then looked over the vase.

"I always loved the way you worked. In order to hide things in plain sight, you create illusions, always aware of the perceptions of others. Cheap fake flowers in a valuable vase to make it appear worthless? Brilliant. I'm going to take this as a down payment."

"It's worth ten grand."

"Perfect. Now. I will let you live on one condition. We both know that your dad's pendant is real and we also know the market value of that little beauty. It will more than make up for the lost girls."

"Much more."

"It's the emotional trauma you're paying me back for."

"That's a lot of trauma for lost cargo."

Kyle leaned in close to Liam. "Let's call it settling a lifetime of debt."

Liam's eyes diverted to the floor. "As much as I'd like to cooperate, you know that my dad and I weren't close. He's dead, and I have no idea where that thing could be. He probably sold it a long time ago."

"You and I both know he didn't steal it for the money."

Liam scoffed. "Everything was about money with my dad."

"Have you forgotten how you went on a rampage to me about how ridiculous he was because you said he was in love with that thing more than anything else in the world, and it represented everything he wasn't. Purity, beauty. You poor, sad creature. But we all have daddy issues. And I would bet my life you know where to get your hands on it, if you haven't already."

"I swear to you, I have no idea where it could be."

"I had hoped it wouldn't come to this. You know how I don't like mixing family with business. Didn't I tell you, Freddy?" Freddy nodded. "But unfortunately, you have given me no choice."

"What's that supposed to mean?"

"It means I know how stubborn you can be, so I took measures to ensure your cooperation." The side of Liam's face twitched. "Your niece."

"Don't you dare."

Kyle shrugged. "It's already done. And you should thank me. I'm only giving you the motivation you require. If you think about it, I'm saving your life because that's the only alternative."

"Let her go and I'll do whatever you want."

"But you were already defeated before you got started. How about we do things my way and we'll get this all over and done with a lot faster."

"Don't do this."

Kyle shrugged. "I've got to protect my business. Besides, if you really can't find it, she won't cover all of my costs, but I'll settle for the emotional damage it will do to you instead. It's your niece or the pendant to pay off the debt. What'll it be?"

"My dad had a house."

"And?"

"He lived there at the end of his life. That's where he died, so his stuff must be there."

"How do you know the house hasn't been sold?"

"Because he left it to me. I own it."

"Aw, that's sweet. So maybe he did care about you a little in the end."

"I'll leave now, but you need to let Sophie go."

"You get me the pendant and I will, but not before." Kyle nodded to Freddy again, who pulled out a knife and cut Liam loose. "Off you go. Better get started. She won't like being held captive, although I intend to treat her like a guest. But if you take too long, I could get bored and mess with her precious little mind."

The twitch of Liam's lip was all the rage that could be seen from the outside. If he had a chance of killing Kyle right there, he would have, but that would get Sophie killed. The first thing he had to find out was if Kyle was messing with him, so he headed straight out the door and jumped on his bike.

Chapter 6

LIAM POUNDED on the door to the split-level ranch. "Claire! Claire, open the door." He closed his eyes to maintain control. He couldn't let his emotions decide how he'd respond. Emotions always led to mistakes and he couldn't afford one mistake on this.

"Liam?" came the voice from within as the door swung open. "Liam, what are you doing here?"

"Is Brian here?"

"No, he's still at work. Won't get home for another hour. Why, is something wrong?"

Liam pushed past his sister and entered the front hall, looking into the living room and then the kitchen, where he saw the pot of pasta sauce he had smelled when he entered. "Sophie. Is she here?"

"No, she stays after school for training. Why?" Fear licked her words.

Liam had worked hard to build a relationship with his sister whom he barely knew growing up. She was ten years older than him and had left home when she was sixteen, but they had reconnected at their father's funeral two years ago. What he hadn't been able to do was ingratiate himself with her husband, who learned about his shady past and was always cold when Liam visited. It had been a delicate balance trying to get to know his sister and niece better while keeping Brian from doing what he really wanted to do. If Kyle had taken Sophie, even if everything worked out in the end, Liam had obliterated any chance that he'd be allowed to see any of them again. But with Sophie's life on the line, nothing else mattered.

"I'm sure everything is fine. I just have to check something. I'll be back." He turned and sprinted for his bike. Claire would worry, but he wasn't prepared to give her the full story until he was certain that the worst had happened. Kyle wasn't one to bluff, but if he hadn't yet followed through on the threat, Liam still a chance that he hadn't completely ruined any future relationship he could have with his only living family. Not until he was sure.

Students were scattered around the side entrance of the school when he arrived. A few checked him out when he approached, but most of them ignored him. He searched the faces and confirmed Sophie wasn't among them.

"Hey." He moved in on the closest student. "Do you know Sophie Turner?"

"Sure. Why? Who are you?"

"I'm her uncle. Have you seen her?"

The student stopped chewing her gum and sized him up, then shrugged. "I saw her around during training, but she's not here now. Ask Melanie over there. They're like best friends."

Liam nodded and jogged over to a girl with short brown hair who was looking at her phone.

"Excuse me, Melanie?" She didn't respond, so he waved a hand in front of her face. She jumped and looked up at him, yanking out an earbud. "What?"

"My name is Liam. I'm Sophie's uncle."

"Okay."

"She was at practice, right?"

"Yeah."

"Have you seen her?"

"Sure, at practice."

Liam wasn't used to people looking at him like he was an idiot, but this girl had made it an art form. "How about after?"

"Nope. Coach made us run at the end of practice. A couple of miles around the block. She was way ahead of me and wasn't here when I got back, so I thought her mom had turned up to get her. I was supposed to give her a lift home. Why? Has something happened?"

"No. No, everything is fine. She, uh, got another lift. I wanted to let you know."

"Then why are you acting so weird?"

"Am I?"

"Yeah."

He shrugged. "Don't know. Maybe it's a grown-up thing?"

"Whatever." She put her earbud back in and lifted her phone.

Liam jogged back to his bike with a million scenarios tossing around in his head. Telling Claire would have to be one of the hardest things he'd ever done in his life.

Claire was out the door before he was even off his bike. She crossed her arms, but when he reached her, she slapped him on the arm. "Why did you do that? Why did you leave me like that? What is going on? Is Sophie okay? Her friend Melanie's mom is supposed to be dropping her off soon."

Liam reached out a hand to put on her arm but pulled it back. She was about to hate his guts. "Can we go inside?"

Claire tripped backward a step. "Don't do that to me. Don't — " Her throat tightened around her words. "Just tell me. Is Sophie okay?"

"I'm sorry, Claire. It's my fault. Sophie's been kidnapped."

The color drained from her face and Liam jumped to catch her before she hit the ground. "Come on. Let me get you inside."

"How could this have happened? How could … I need to call Brian. He needs to come home."

Liam helped her to the couch. "Do you want me to call him?"

"No." She looked up at him. "He doesn't trust you."

She shook her head, then studied her fingers as she picked at the nail beds.

He could almost read her thoughts that maybe her husband had been right all along to be suspicious of Liam. "I'm so sorry, Claire, but I promise you I will make it right."

"But I don't understand? Why would someone take Sophie? Why would they do that? Why her?"

He wouldn't tell her the details of the human trafficking. That would be too much. "They want something from me that they knew I wouldn't want to give them. They thought if they took her, then I would do whatever they wanted. And they were right."

"So give it to them. Why haven't you given it to them?"

"I don't have it yet, but I can promise you, I'll get it and I'll bring Sophie home to you safe. I promise." As the word *promise* came out a second time, he flinched. Lying was so easy for him. Even to those he cared about the most.

"So what is it? What do they want?"

"Something of dad's. Something he had a long time ago. It will be at his house in New York."

"What is it?"

"You remember that flower pendant?"

"I don't know. That may have been after I left."

"Oh, right. Well, it's worth a lot of money."

"That's all they want? Money? We have some — "

"No, it's worth a lot more than what you have. Trust me."

"So these are guys who knew Dad? But if it was worth so much money, wouldn't Dad have sold it?"

"No. That pendant was really important to him."

"Don't be ridiculous. Nothing was important to him."

"Trust me. It was the one thing he never would have parted with. Not for any amount of money."

"I hope you're right."

"I am."

Claire bit her lip. "So, this isn't about you, then? You said you weren't involved in any of that stuff anymore, but this is about Dad?" She looked up at him, her eyes pleading for the truth, hoping that the truth was what she wanted to hear.

Liam was torn between giving her what she wanted and giving her what he argued with himself that she needed. "Yeah. It's the past. It's caught up with us. I'm sorry."

That settled Claire a little, but the lie twisted knots in his stomach. "So you have to go to New York?"

"Yeah."

"We should call the police."

"No. We can't. We can't risk it. I don't know where they're holding her. If these guys get a whiff of police involvement, it could endanger Soph's life even more. The only way to get her back is to make sure they get what they want." Or, if Liam couldn't find what they wanted, he'd do whatever it took to get her back or die trying.

"Okay. If you think that's best." A tremor ran through Claire's body, and she pressed her hands between her knees to settle it. "You know how to handle this stuff way better than I do. Wait. Brian. I don't know if he'll go along with it."

"Go along with what?" came a deep voice from the door. "What are you doing here, Liam?"

Claire jumped up to stand between her husband and her brother. "Wait, please. Hear him out."

"You have some nerve turning up here when you're in trouble. Don't think I'll bail you out. If you made a mess, you need to clean it up yourself. Don't get my family involved in your business."

Liam moved around his sister to face his accuser. He had no other choice. "Sophie's been kidnapped. I'm trying to save her."

Brian bounded forward and punched Liam in the head. Liam allowed the force of the misguided punch to send him to his knees. He could have easily dodged it, but he knew Brian needed the satisfaction. What he wasn't expecting was for Brian to kick him in the ribs once he was down.

Claire screamed for Brian to stop as she pushed him aside when he went for a second kick. Then she clamped her hand over her mouth. This was a respectable suburb, and a howling neighbor could warrant a concerned call to 911. "Please stop it. Liam is our only chance of getting Sophie back."

Liam got to his feet and Brian pointed a thick finger at him. "You stay where you are, you psycho. I'm calling the cops, and after they take you to jail, they can go get our little girl back."

Liam's lips flattened as he prepared for what he

knew he had to do. Brian wouldn't listen to reason while fear and anger fueled him. This would not end well.

As soon as Brian put his hand into his pocket to retrieve his cell, Liam lunged forward and punched him in the stomach. It was easy to slip the phone from him and guide him to the couch while Brian struggled to take a breath. Claire was hyperventilating.

"I'm so … " What could he say? "You have to understand, if you call the cops, then Sophie's as good as dead. Please let me do this. I don't want to hurt you, but I can't risk Sophie's life."

Brian had gotten his breath back. "You can't risk it? You son of a — " Brian pounced and Liam used the other man's weight to send him crashing into the coffee table. He heard a crack and hoped it was the wood.

"Stay down, Brian. You can't win this fight. I'm just trying to fix the mistake I made. If you call the police, she's as good as dead. You have to trust me."

"I've never trusted you." His eyes shot over to Claire. "I told you what he was, but you wouldn't listen and now look what's happened."

Claire was crying. "I just want my baby back."

"I know you think I'm a monster, and maybe you're right."

"I am right."

"But I know how these guys work, and I'm your best way of getting her back. You don't have to like it, but it's the truth. And once Sophie is safe, you never have to see me again."

Brian ran a hand through his dark hair as he stood.

"You get her back and if so much as a hair on her head is out of place, I will hunt you down and kill you."

"She'll be okay. I promise." Liam turned for the door and Claire started to follow, but Brian grabbed her arm. "I don't want you anywhere near him."

Liam didn't hear his sister's response, but as much as he would mourn the loss of his family, he knew it was for the best. They didn't need him in their lives, not if this was the consequence.

When he reached his bike, Claire called out to him, and he turned in surprise.

She stumbled down to the road. "My poor baby. She must be so terrified."

Liam squeezed her arm. "They won't hurt her."

"Are you sure? Can you really know that?"

"Yes. It would jeopardize them getting what they want. They'll want to make sure she's looked after."

"What if the pendant isn't there? What will they do if it isn't there?"

"It will be. I told you, he never would have sold it."

"But what if you can't find it?"

"I will."

Claire was too desperate not to believe him. "Okay. I can hang on for a day or two."

"Good. You'll do great. And like I said. It will all be okay."

Claire nodded. "And I'll be praying too."

Liam jerked back. "What?"

"I'll pray. Sophie and I have been going to church. It's new to us, but I do believe that God can help. I can ask some of the others to pray too. I won't tell them what. They're always saying they don't need to know because God knows."

God was the last person Liam wanted involved. He'd likely strike Liam down dead for the things he'd done. He'd prefer to keep God out of it, but if it gave Claire comfort, then he'd stay out of it.

"I'll get going then. I'll let you know when I find it."

Chapter 7

EMILY PULLED her truck up to the curb outside a quaint little cottage. The flowerpots that always hung on the porch during the spring and summer hadn't been put up yet, even though they'd had a few warmer days. But that didn't diminish the charm of the place. The Carsons didn't have much money, but Mrs. Carson sure had style.

Emily propped open the white picket fence in preparation for her delivery, then she walked up the marbly path, stepping off onto the grass before she arrived at the steps. She loved the cushiony grass but didn't stray off the path too long. They had the best lawn in town, but Mr. Carson had a thing about people walking on it.

After the brief detour into the forbidden yard, she rapped her knuckles on the door. "Special delivery!" she called out, knowing her voice would need to reach Mrs. Carson, who was most likely sitting at the kitchen table doing her cryptic crossword and sipping a cup of tea.

She knocked again for good measure, then turned to

breathe deeply of the warming air that still held a crisp edge.

"Coming," sang a soft voice from within.

When the door opened, a small woman with white hair pulled into a bun peered at Emily through her Coke-bottle glasses. She tapped Emily on the leg with her cane before taking her hand in a surprisingly strong grip and pulling her down for a hug. Emily nearly toppled forward as she leaned over to embrace the woman.

"Emily, we are so excited to see the treasure you have created for us." Mrs. Carson stiffened. "Oh!"

"What is it? Are you okay?"

"Risks."

"Risks?"

"Takes a chance, right, and skis off."

"Pardon?"

Mrs. Carson turned and scrambled back to the kitchen. "Five letters. Ha ha!"

"I'm confused," Emily called out as she followed the old woman.

"The answer is *risks*."

"Oh, your crossword."

She rapped a knuckle on her head. "Good for the noggin', the cryptic."

"Wouldn't know."

"Now that that's settled, let's have a look at what you've brought."

"I hope you like them. Sixty years married is something to really celebrate."

"We will love them, dear. Do you need some help?

Do you need me to get Roger? He's been on the toilet for nearly an hour. It's time for him to do some actual work."

Emily was accustomed to Mrs. Carson saying whatever she liked, but Emily couldn't help the blush that crept up her neck.

"It's fine. Leave Roger where he is. I can carry these. I'll just bring them in one at a time."

After Emily had put the two tables in their appropriate spaces on each side of the bed, she stood back to admire how well they suited the room. She was especially proud of the curved feature on the two drawers that acted as handles. They reminded her of an ash leaf, even though the pieces were made of walnut.

Mrs. Carson breathed out a long sigh. "They're perfect." She paid as much attention to the bedroom as she did her garden and even after studying the room to get a sense for what the right piece might be, Emily had been apprehensive until she got Mrs. Carson's approval.

"They do look nice in here."

"Perfect fit." Mrs. Carson pressed a fist up to her mouth.

"That is quite the compliment coming from someone with your defined taste. I'm pleased they work so well."

A hacking cough and a grumble preceded the entrance of Mr. Carson, who had finally joined them.

He hiked up his trousers before speaking. "What's this?"

"Oh, Roger. Aren't they wonderful?"

"What?"

"The new nightstands Emily created for us."

"What, those? I could have knocked up something like that with a few bits of pine I have out in the back shed." He sniffed.

Emily smiled. She'd known these two since she was a little girl and had learned over the years that Roger was physically incapable of giving a compliment. But she'd also learned that the worse he spoke about something, the more he admired it.

"I hope you don't hate them too much, Mr. Carson."

"As long as it doesn't collapse when I set a glass of water on it, I guess it will do."

"Oh, Roger. Stop it. They're perfect."

"All I'm saying is that they better be properly built. These days everything falls apart in less than a year. I like my stuff to last."

"Don't worry. It will hold your water for many years to come."

"Good, 'cuz I get thirsty at night and I don't want to walk all the way to the kitchen for a drink." With that, he turned and left the two women to continue their appraisal.

"Oh, before you go, hun." Mrs. Carson moved in close, her cane coming perilously close to squashing Emily's toe. "You weren't up at Richard Hargrave's place last night, were you?"

"Last night? No, I don't go up there at night. Why?"

"That's what I thought. I know how much you love

it up there, but I heard from my neighbor, Wendy. She drove past the house. Well, not past it, but you know, down at the bottom of the road? She was on her way to the pharmacy because her daughter, Susan, came down with the flu, and she had to go on a late-night run to get some medicine. That's when she drove by. But I think she got the name brand."

"What?"

"She could have gotten the generic brand. It's cheaper."

"Oh, the medicine."

"I always get the generic brand. Why pay more for the same thing? 'Cause you know it's the same thing. They want to take your money for nothin'. But you know Wendy. She's not as careful as some of us who don't have money to throw around. I know her husband has a good job and all, but it's like throwing money in the garbage, if you ask me."

Emily pressed her tongue to the roof of her mouth, trying to stay patient with Mrs. Carson's meandering. "Did she see something at the house?"

"Yes. She said she saw a light. Like a flashlight beam casting about the place."

"Really?"

"Do you think we should call the police?"

"Probably just be some local kids looking for a place to hang out, but I'd hate to see that house get more ruined than it already is. I'll have a look and call the police if I think it's necessary."

"Thanks, dear. You're a real treasure, you know that?"

Emily offered Mrs. Carson a tight-lipped smile and headed for the door.

"Can I get you a cup of tea before you go?"

"I'd love one, but I'll have to save it for another time. I've got a lot to do today."

"Okay, well, thanks again and we'll see you Sunday."

"Yes, you will. See you then."

Emily yanked her truck door shut harder than necessary and gripped the steering wheel until her knuckles were white. If some local kids were messing around up at the house, she'd soon put a stop to it. There were lots of other places in town where they could get into trouble, but she wouldn't let her favorite place be treated like a playhouse.

She started the truck and headed straight for Richard's house. If anyone was there last night, there would be evidence. And if she was lucky, maybe they'd still be around. She wouldn't mind catching the culprits red-handed. Otherwise she could always set up cameras to catch them in the act.

Staying on the side of caution, she parked at the end of the driveway, out of sight. If the intruders were still at the house, she wanted the element of surprise.

She snuck up behind some overgrown bushes close to the house to listen but jumped when the screen door slapped on the frame.

Still there. Half of her mouth lifted in a smirk.

She crouched down and crept to the side of the

house, peeking around the corner and up to the porch, but whoever it was had gone inside.

She put a hand to the back of her jeans and pulled out her phone, getting ready to take photographic evidence, then she hurried around the front of the porch, keeping herself out of view.

On the other side of the house was a large window that looked through the living room and into the kitchen.

With her head tipped to the side, she twisted it around just enough to peek inside. The intruder was bent over, looking in a box. When he straightened, with his back to her, he put his hands on his hips.

This was not a kid. This was a man with dark hair and broad shoulders. She took a quick picture and gritted her teeth. Richard's stuff wasn't there for some treasure hunter. She moved past the window, then sprinted to the back of the house where she spotted a motorcycle. It was parked under a large beech tree at the back of the house.

She continued to the nearby shed and grabbed a shovel, yanking it from where it had settled into the ground. But before racing back to the house, she took a closer look at the bike.

She could smash it. It would serve him right, whoever this guy was. But she'd save that as a plan B. She had an eye for craftsmanship and even though she didn't know much about bikes, it was obvious that this was something special and didn't deserve to be destroyed simply because of its owner.

Liam had been through every box in the house. Twice. After a frantic search when he'd arrived in the early hours of the morning, he finally collapsed into a heap after riding ten hours through the night. Not only had Kyle slashed the tires of his car, but there were no flights for twenty-four hours, so he had jumped on his bike. The first couple of hours did him some good, but after that it was a strain.

Now, he'd spent the entire morning rechecking boxes and drawers and all the obvious hiding places like the toilet cisterns. But his dad had always been good at finding unusual hiding spots. The man trusted no one and always assumed his enemy was smarter than him. It's probably what kept him alive for so long.

He put his hands on his hips and sighed up at the ceiling. The next step was to pull the house itself apart, but the property was larger than he'd first thought. His dad had had good taste in his choice. The views were probably better than anywhere else in town. It was the sort of place he could see himself retiring to one day, if he ever got that far. But he'd do whatever it took to get his hands on that pendant, even if it meant tearing up every board in the house.

In one last attempt to discover the pendant, he went back to the dusty bureau, the only decent piece of furniture in the house. After carefully checking inside each drawer, including looking for hiding places, he finally gave up, but his fingers lingered on the intricate pattern on the edge of the top before his arm retreated to his side. He needed to take a break, and that view out the front called to him.

He dragged his feet across the porch until his toe caught on a loose board. He stomped it down, then leaned on a pillar with his arms crossed.

The buds pushing out of the branches in the nearby trees brought a brief smile to his lips. He loved the city, but being in a place like this, with the smell of green and a chill in the air that was fresh, reminded him of Peter's place. A little of that peace he felt out there was in this place too.

When Emily heard the thwack of the screen again, she hurried to get into position with the shovel held like a baseball bat.

She readied herself at the corner of the house, listening to the scrape of feet on the weathered boards. The intruder was definitely on the porch this time. Her porch.

After several steadying breaths, she gripped the handle tighter, then stepped silently out from her hiding place.

The man stood facing the other direction, looking out over the view. She shifted her hands as though a different grip would make any difference and inched closer. If he was dangerous, it would be better to incapacitate him before he knew she was there, but if he was dangerous, then she should retreat and call the cops.

Her indecision toyed with her mind, but she still

moved forward, putting a foot on the lower step. He was close enough that if she swung now, she could catch him in the knee and drop him. Or she could step back and get his attention. It made more sense to simply ask who he was and what he was doing there. If it was all a misunderstanding, she'd regret using attack as her first approach. But the fear that played on her mind wanted to end the threat before it became one.

Then he shifted on his feet, and she panicked.

Chapter 8

A CREAK from behind sent Liam's senses ablaze and his muscles tensed. He turned in time to see the shovel swinging toward his knees. He dropped low enough so his thigh took most of the hit. He grabbed the shovel and pulled it from his assailant's hands.

The woman squealed and jumped back, tripping on the step and falling hard onto her butt.

Liam jumped from the porch with the shovel raised and ready to strike. The woman screamed and covered herself as best as she could. "Wait! Stop!"

He backed up, the shovel still raised, but with no intention of using it for anything but intimidation. Kyle wouldn't have sent someone so incompetent. This woman did not know what she was doing.

"Are you going to hit me?"

The smile that appeared on Liam's face at the absurdity of the situation brought a scowl to the woman's.

This was somewhat of a new experience for him, dealing with an amateur. He wasn't quite sure how to proceed. But when she kept herself twisted in what looked like a very uncomfortable defensive position, he gave her a break and stuck the shovel into the ground.

"I won't hit you."

The woman waited. For what, he wasn't sure. If he was going to attack, he would have done it already.

He leaned on the shovel. "I promise." He winked and her frown deepened.

She slowly unwound herself and scooted backward before jumping to her feet and stepping back so that he couldn't reach her. Or so she thought.

"So, are you going to tell me why you tried to break my legs?"

His casual manner riled her. "You're trespassing."

"Oh." This should be interesting. "Am I?" Maybe this was the distraction he needed to clear his head.

Emily crossed her arms against the stranger whose complete dismissal of her was mildly infuriating but completely eradicated her fear somehow. He was one of those guys who was good-looking and knew it. He used his charm as the easiest way to get what he wanted, but she wouldn't let him out of this one.

"Don't get smart with me," she said. "This is my town and I know what goes on around here. You are an intruder." Every syllable that came out of her mouth sounded corny, and unfortunately, judging by the smirk on the man's face, he thought so too. She tried to ignore the heat creeping up her neck.

"So, this is your property, then?"

"Yes. No. I mean, I'm the caretaker. I look after it for a friend."

"The owner?"

She lifted her chin a little higher. "Yes."

"How do you know the owner hasn't invited me here?"

She scoffed. "Nice try. Look. If you don't voluntarily leave this property, I'll have to call the police." She tried to say the last part with as much sass as she could muster, but the way he looked at her made her feel like she was in middle school.

"Okay."

"Okay, you'll leave? Or, okay, call the police?"

"Call the cops."

"Fine, if that's what you want."

"It is."

"Fine. You think I won't call your bluff?" She pulled her phone out of her pocket and growled, then held it up for him to see. "Look what you made me do. It's smashed now."

"I made you take a swing at me?" He shook his head and pulled his own phone out of his pocket, unlocking it. "Call on my phone then."

He tossed it to her, and she bobbled it before she got it securely in her grasp.

She saw a picture of a woman, about forty, and a teenage girl before she glanced up at him. He was too young for that to be his family.

She planted her hand on her hip while she made the call. He was playing some kind of game with her, stalling for time or expecting her to give up and leave him alone. But there was nothing he could do to make her back down now. She was committed to seeing him run out of town. Some things she hated about a small town, but it had its perks. Like the fact that everyone would be on her side in this.

Liam watched her make the call after tucking her hair behind her ear. She was pretty in a small-town sort of way. You rarely saw a smattering of freckles on a grown woman, and she had a spark about her he'd never come across.

"Stevie, hey, I'm glad you're the one who answered. It's Emily … yeah, no, my phone's broken. This is someone else's. Look, I need you to get up to Richard's place … yes, it is police business. There is an intruder on the property and he refuses to leave … yes, I'm safe." She looked up at Liam and took another step back. "Yeah. We'll wait. See you soon." She hung up the phone and threw it back at him. Harder than necessary. He caught it one-handed without a blink.

"You're welcome," he said.

"I didn't say thank you."

"Even criminals deserve manners."

"Oh, so you admit you're a criminal?"

"I won't lie and say I'm a saint. So, how long do we have to wait for Stevie to turn up? I've got things to do."

"His name is Officer Steve Ridel, and you can leave now if you want."

"That's generous."

"We don't have to make this painful."

"I'll take my chances. So you guys are pals, then? You and Officer Ridel?"

"Everybody knows everybody around here. And we protect each other."

"Sounds suffocating."

She opened her mouth to fire a shot but paused before responding. "Maybe, but it comes in handy."

"Huh."

"What?"

"Nothin'. I've just never lived in a small town before."

"So, what are you doing here now? Looking for a place to crash? How'd you even know the house was vacant? There are plenty of places in the city you could find. Why not head there? Why stop here?"

"You sure have a lot of questions."

"I think they are valid questions that I have a right to ask."

"Oh, right. As the caretaker of the property. How much you get paid for something like that?"

She scrunched up her nose, exaggerating the freckles. "That's none of your business."

"So a lot, then?"

The crunch of tires on the driveway had her standing up straighter, but she didn't turn her back on him to check the arrival of the police car. His gaze lifted over her shoulder.

"This is your last chance," she said. "You can leave

on your own two feet or be escorted in the back of a police car."

"I'll take my chances." He walked toward her and she scrambled sideways before slamming her hands onto her hips when he ambled past, heading for the police car.

Stevie, a baby-faced officer with sandy hair, got out of his patrol car, keeping his eye on the stranger as he strolled forward with his hands resting on his belt.

"This him?" he asked Emily.

"Yes, it is." She crossed her arms in victory.

Stevie said, "Sir, I have been informed by this young lady that there is a trespasser on the property."

"Correct," Liam said.

Stevie's eyes flicked sideways to Emily, then back to Liam. "So, you admit to trespassing?"

"No sir, but I would like to report that this young lady is trespassing on my property and that she assaulted me with the intention to harm."

"What?" Emily choked.

Stevie's mouth collapsed into a frown that Liam couldn't quite interpret.

Liam turned to Emily to break the bad news, enjoying every second of it. "This is my house, and you not only trespassed, but you also assaulted me." Liam didn't miss the movement of Stevie's hand, which now rested on his gun. "Small towns," Liam mumbled.

Emily took an aggressive step forward. "What did you say?"

"What I said was that Officer Ridel is not pleased to find out that I might be the good guy in all of this."

"You might be something, but you are definitely not the good guy here."

"Emily. Is this true? Did you assault him?" Stevie asked.

"N — Yes." Stevie let out a sigh that, to Liam, sounded like he wasn't surprised.

Liam grinned. "Don't tell me you make a habit out of attacking strangers." The fear he saw enter her eyes surprised him enough to wipe the smile off his face, but she recovered quickly.

"I didn't even hurt you. Admit it."

Liam rubbed his leg. "I think there might be a bruise." His frown turned coy when Stevie pressed his hand to his eyes.

Emily growled. "I don't know who you think you are — "

"Hang on a second," Stevie said, stepping between the two who had moved quite close. "This is getting out of hand. Would you please both come down to the station so we can get this sorted out down there?"

"Absolutely," Emily said, and stomped off for her truck.

"You're not going to arrest her for the assault?"

Stevie opened his mouth but didn't have a response. Liam chuckled. "I'm only kidding. If you're happy for me to ride my bike down, I'll meet you there."

"Uh. Yeah. Um."

"See you there."

Stevie sighed before getting into his own vehicle. With Emily, nothing was ever simple.

Chapter 9

WHEN LIAM ARRIVED at the police station, Emily was already seated. Her body language was smug. The straight back and aloof grin were like fuel to the fire for a guy like him. He thought back to the fear he had seen and wondered if he'd misinterpreted. Everything about this woman said she was a spoiled brat, used to getting her own way. But that was fine with Liam. He didn't mind putting someone in their place when necessary. It would ease his stress.

The chairs were close together, and he sat right next to her, forcing her to lean away.

He put an elbow on each arm rest and smiled, content.

Emily considered moving but didn't like how he controlled everything. From the beginning, her whole encounter with him was on his terms, so she stayed where she was.

"It might interest you to know that I ran a politician out of town once."

He looked at her with feigned interest. "Is that so?"

"Yeah. He turned up acting all smarmy, kinda like you are now, making promises he had no intention of keeping."

"How do you know he was lying?"

"He was only here to have an affair with the bank manager."

"And that makes him a liar?"

"It does when he cops a feel of me in line at the grocery store."

"That makes him a sleaze, not a liar."

"To me, they're the same."

"But what you're saying is you ran him out of town because of his election speech, not because he's a pig?"

"My point is, if you're not who you say you are, consider yourself gone."

"Thanks for the heads-up."

"One more piece of important information."

"I'm listening."

"I personally know the owner of that house, and you are not him."

"Knew."

"Pardon me?"

"You knew the owner of that house. He's dead."

"How'd you know that? Did you look back through obituaries to find an unoccupied house you could move into?"

“Not a bad idea, actually. But you wouldn’t try it in a small town. And not two years later. But in a highly populated area? Yeah. It could work.”

“Oh, right, so you’re an expert then?” She pinched her lips closed when she realized how loud her voice was.

Stevie came out from the back. He strolled over slowly, getting a good look at the two. Liam appeared to be amused by Emily’s anger. He couldn’t blame him, the way her nose scrunched up. It was one of the things that had attracted him to her in high school. Unfortunately for Liam, the carefree full-of-himself attitude would not work on her. She was not one to be charmed.

“Am I interrupting?”

“Not at all,” Emily said. “What have you got for us?”

“I’ve called the lawyer that dealt with Mr. Hargrave’s estate and asked him to look into this situation.”

“Great,” Liam said, offering Emily an enormous grin. He couldn’t imagine what was so important to her about that house, especially when someone like his dad had lived there, but she would not like it if she found out he was going to tear it apart.

“Emily?” Stevie said, leaning toward her. “Can I speak with you for a moment?”

“Sure.” She followed him over to the watercooler. “I

hope you brought me over here to tell me some good news."

He bit his lip. "We've been friends for a long time."

"Yes, we have," she said, now cautious.

"I know you love that place, but even if this Liam guy isn't who he says he is, you are, in fact, trespassing. Richard doesn't own that house anymore."

"Oh, come on. Are you serious?"

"It's just … You need to be careful. Normally it wouldn't matter, but it could become a very big problem if the owner turns up and wants to press charges. Especially if Liam is the owner."

"Liam's not going to press charges."

"You did assault him."

"I was protecting myself."

"On his property?"

"Don't tell me you can't see through that. He's buying himself time."

"Emily, that's not what he's doing. When I spoke to the lawyer, he told me it was Richard's son who inherited the property."

"Yeah, I already knew that, but you can't tell me this is him."

Stevie scratched his head. "His name is Liam Hargrave."

"It's not that uncommon of a name. And who knows if his ID is even real?"

"Emily."

"Stevie, come on."

"Why is it so hard to believe that Liam could be Richard's son?"

"Because he can't be. Richard's son is off climbing Mount Everest."

"Emily."

"Richard's son wouldn't be so arrogant."

"No?"

She pushed her fingers against her temple. "You really think that's him?"

"I do. I'm working with the lawyer to confirm it, but it's the only thing that makes sense. If he were some guy off the street, he'd be long gone. Trust me. There is no way he'd be willing to face your wrath unless he was confident in his position."

Emily pulled a flimsy plastic cup from the cart beside her, filling it and tipping it back before she spoke. "Do you think he'll press charges?"

"You haven't been very nice to him."

She clicked her tongue. "It was a misunderstanding."

"Fine, go tell him that. I'd hate to arrest you."

"Oh, stop it. It won't come to that."

"I hope not." Stevie lifted his eyebrows. "I'll check with the lawyer. See how things are coming along."

Emily stayed facing away from Liam until Stevie had disappeared again. She poured herself another cup of water, trying to buy herself a few precious seconds before she'd have to go humble herself to this egotistical stranger whose name happened to be Liam Hargrave.

God, please don't let him press charges.

She crumpled up the cup, tossing it into the garbage before turning. Keeping her eyes glued to the floor, she made her way back to Liam and sat down, making sure her arm didn't brush his as she slid onto the narrow chair.

"You two have a nice chat?" he asked.

She didn't look at him, fearing that the smug look she knew he wore would be enough to keep her from doing what she knew she had to do. "I'd like to apologize for hitting you with the shovel. If you really are the owner of that house, then I am sorry for the misunderstanding."

"You can't say it like you mean it? I mean, I know you don't. I know this is killing you. But I thought you'd give it a bit more effort."

She pressed her lips together and swallowed back all the things she desperately wanted to say, then counted to ten and said through her teeth, "I only thought I was protecting the house."

"By trespassing?"

She closed her eyes. Her hand lifted unconsciously to grasp the pendant at her chest, slipping it out from under her shirt.

Liam locked eyes on the necklace and almost swore. He'd been handed a miracle.

"I'm just trying to ap — "

"Hey, listen, don't sweat it."

Her eyes opened wide. "What?"

"It's no big deal. I was just giving you a hard time."

"What? Why?"

He shrugged. "'Cause you caught me off guard."

"But you … I don't understand."

He turned his body toward her to give the appearance of genuine concern. "Look, Emily. I know — Hey, that's a pretty necklace."

Her hand grabbed at the pendant.

"It's special, I take it? Or … "

Emily lifted the pendant to look at it. "Not that it's any of your business, but yes, it's important to me."

"That's too bad."

"Why?"

"I was looking for something special to give to my grandmother. She'd love it. I don't suppose … "

"No. It's not for sale."

"Not for any price?"

"No." She tucked the necklace back in her shirt.

Not as easy as he'd hoped. He'd have to change his tact. "Anyway, thanks for looking after my place. I really do appreciate it, even if it didn't sound that way at the start. You're welcome anytime." He smiled his million-dollar smile. It was the one he never had to practice because he was born with it. It carried warmth, joy, and passion, and it said to the receiver that they had broken through his tough exterior.

A crease formed between her eyes. Not the usual response he got.

"You don't make any sense."

"What do you mean?"

"You threaten to have me arrested and then suddenly we're best buddies?"

"I got carried away?"

"No. You're up to something. I just don't know what."

This would take time. If he'd known she had the pendant from the start, things would have gone very differently. Now he'd have to make up the ground.

Emily stood. "I'm going to get another drink of water."

She hovered by the watercooler, not willing to look his way.

He watched her, making the usual assessments about her characteristics, adding assumptions about her hopes and dreams that he'd try to get concrete information on. Normally, he'd spend weeks or even months researching a mark, but he didn't have that kind of time. Ultimately, he'd do whatever it took to get that necklace from around Emily's neck. Sophie's life depended on it. But right now, all he could do was make a list and prepare. The good news was, he now knew where it was. That was news too good not to share.

Liam went outside for some air and called his sister. "Claire." He could hear her hyperventilating. "Everything is fine. I'm calling you with good news."

"Oh, thank goodness. You found it. Are you on your way home?"

"No, not yet."

"Why not?"

"I know where it is. I've found it, but I don't have my hands on it yet."

"That doesn't even make any sense. You're saying you've seen it, but you can't take it?"

"You'll just have to trust me that it's complicated."

"Someone else has it?"

"Yes."

"For crying out loud, Liam. You, of all people, should know how to get something from someone. Did you grow a conscience when I wasn't looking?" That hurt him, but he deserved it. "Go find whoever it is and take it."

"If I could, I would."

"Do they know how much it's worth? Can we buy it from them?"

"No. But I promise you, I am handling it. I will get it. You need to trust me."

"I do trust you, Liam. It's just, sometimes I wonder if you've looked at all of your options or if you're just doing the only thing you know to do."

"I would never put Sophie's life more at risk. Hang in there. You'll have her back soon."

Claire let out a shaky breath. "I'm trying to hang in there, but it's not easy. Every time I close my eyes, I see my little girl in trouble."

"She's not. I promise."

"Thank you for saying that, but how can you be sure?"

Liam pressed his fingers into his eyes. "Just hang in there, okay? I'll see if I can get some assurance for you."

"Can you do that?"

"I can try."

Liam slouched in the chair again, waiting for matters to be settled. Emily refused to come near him again, which gave him a sick feeling that this would be one con he wouldn't be able to see through. And it happened to be the most important one of his life.

He wouldn't approach her again, not without more information. As much as he wanted to rush this, he couldn't. He had been flying blind with her before and it had backfired, and he wouldn't make the same mistake again. So even though it was another hour before the matter was settled, he let her keep to herself.

Stevie shook both their hands after confirming Liam was who he said he was, and Emily breezed by him without another look.

Liam waited behind. "Officer Ridel, do you have a minute?"

"Sure."

"I wanted to thank you for taking the time to sort all of this out. I know it would have been easier to arrest me."

"I don't arrest anyone who doesn't deserve it."

"But you must be very busy, and I want you to know that it means a lot."

"No need to thank me. I'm just doing my job."

Want to get something personal? Offer something personal. "I think I got a little carried away with Emily. It's" — he ran a hand through his hair — "it's been emotional visiting my dad's house again. After he died, I couldn't face that place for a long time. Too many demons. And

I'm finding, now that I'm here, it brings back a lot of things."

"Yeah, I imagine it would."

Now time for the transition. "Did you know my dad at all?"

"Not really. Emily knew him pretty well, but I only knew him to look at."

"I guess you know Emily, though? You think she'll be okay? I really didn't mean to get under her skin like I did. It's a bit of a defense mechanism I have."

"She'll be fine. You might have cracked her cool exterior, but she's been through tougher stuff. She'll probably give you the cold shoulder if she sees you around town, but she'll get over it. I appreciate it that you chose not to press charges. She really likes that house. She was genuinely trying to protect it."

"Yeah, I'm glad to know it was looked after while I couldn't be here. And I'm grateful you turned up when you did. I'm afraid we're both stubborn enough that things could have gotten ugly."

"Glad we got it sorted."

"Hey, what did you mean when you said she's been through tougher stuff? Seems to me like she's got the whole town looking after her. She told me the story about running the politician out of town."

"She told you about that?"

"Yeah, that must have been something. Did you all get your pitchforks and torches and chase him out together?"

Stevie frowned. "So she didn't tell you?"

"Yeah, she said he was a liar and was having an

affair with the bank manager before he grabbed her in the grocery store."

"But she didn't tell you what happened?"

"I thought that was everything. Was there more?"

"I guess I'm not telling you anything everyone doesn't already know." He looked at the floor. "When he touched her at the store, she had a sort of meltdown."

"What is a 'sort of' meltdown?"

"She freaked. Spun out, screaming at him right there in front of everyone."

"Wow."

"Yeah."

"What do you think brought that on? I mean, it sounds like there's a past."

"Oh yeah, there's something there. Before all that, she had moved into the city."

"You mean New York?"

"Yeah. She makes high-end furniture. At least, she used to. Tried to make it in the big city. Everyone here thought she was doing great. I mean, that's what it sounded like."

"But she wasn't?"

"Who knows? Her mom died, and she came home saying she was there because her dad needed help."

"But you don't think that's why?"

"I always thought she ran from something in the city that needed to be left."

"What do you mean?"

"Can't say for sure. But there's a haunted look in her eye that wasn't there before and the security she has set up at her place … " He shook his head. "It's like

Fort Knox. You don't do that 'cause you lost your mom."

So, no breaking into the house then. With all the easy options now removed, it was up to Liam to do what he did best. It would just take the longest. He'd need more information. "I'm sorry to hear her mom passed away. That must have been hard."

"It was complicated and no secret that she and her mom didn't get along well. They were two very hard-headed women, and her mom's drinking problem made things worse. But again, I'm not telling you anything the whole town doesn't already know."

This whole small-town thing worked out really well for him. Maybe that's why his dad settled here, because it was such an easy place to work. He almost felt sorry for Emily. He'd know her whole life story before long.

"I guess you know her pretty well." He rubbed his hand on the back of his neck, pretending that he was uncomfortable asking the next question. "You, uh, you guys ever a thing? I thought I saw something there."

Stevie chuckled. "No way. In high school, I had a huge crush on her, but I've come to my senses. She's way too much for someone like me. I know she lives here in this small town, but she's made for bigger things."

"Yeah, I kinda got that vibe from her."

"No one was surprised when she left. It's actually sad that she came back and stayed."

"Now I feel terrible treating her the way I did."

"She'll be fine. Don't give yourself that much credit." They shared a laugh.

"Maybe. But do you think she'd let me take her out

to dinner or something to say sorry?"

"You mean like a date?"

Liam noticed a slight look of horror on Stevie's face. "No, nothing like that. Just a genuine apology."

"As long as it's not a date."

"I don't mean to step on your toes. I thought — "

"No, it's not that. Whatever it was that caused her to respond to being groped that day has put up a big wall around her. If she thinks you're asking her out … well, I can't be held responsible for the consequences. Now that you know, make sure you're careful with her."

"Thanks, Stevie. Truly." Liam tipped his head and turned to leave.

"Oh, and Liam?"

"Yeah?"

"Welcome to Oakridge."

Liam smiled and headed out the door with his phone in his hand.

He had one more call he had to make.

"I hope you've got good news for me, Liam."

"I do. I found the pendant."

"Great. Excellent work. You let me know when you're back in town and we'll organize a swap."

"I said I found it. I didn't say I have it."

"So what's the holdup?"

"It got complicated. It's not at my dad's house. He gave it to someone. I have to get it back."

"I'm sorry, Liam, are you saying there's a problem? Just go over to this person's house and take it. It's a small town. Most people leave their doors unlocked, don't they?"

"Not this one. I've already checked. The house is locked up tight."

"Great. I'll send a team, help you out."

"No. I'll get it."

"Liam, I want that pendant."

"All I need is a little more time. And I want assurances that Sophie's okay."

"Is this a joke? You call me up to tell me you're going to be late with your payment and then have the cheek to ask me for something?"

"You never put a time limit on our arrangement."

Liam heard Kyle's long sigh as he considered Liam's request. "I feel like you'd be more motivated if I make you suffer."

"It's not for me. I need to show my sister that she doesn't have to call the police. She's not doing well."

"Fine. I'll take some video and get it to you. But, Liam, remember that everything can change in an instant."

"I know."

The phone went dead and Liam closed his eyes. He tried to convince himself that the knot in his stomach was due solely to Sophie, but hearing about Emily pricked at his conscience in ways he wasn't prepared for. But the last thing he could afford to do was let it become personal.

When he jumped on his bike and started the engine, he resolved himself to his task. He'd done the same thing hundreds of times, and Emily was no different.

Chapter 10

EMILY BLEW a gust of air toward her forehead to remove a stray lock of hair that hung over her eye. The smile that had been plastered on her face dropped away as soon as she turned from the table she had been serving. She hated waiting on tables more than anything.

It wasn't that she minded the people, but growing up, it had been her duty to serve at the restaurant when she wasn't at school. It meant that when her friends would come in on the weekends stuffing their faces and having a good time, her only option was to work. She swore she'd never do it again. But everyone in town knew that she'd come home from the city to help her dad, and whether or not it was the truth, she'd grin and bear it for her dad while half the staff was home with the flu.

Apparently, the virus hadn't reached any other part of the population. That morning had been the busiest yet. Now that they were closing in on lunchtime, the line had only just dwindled down to a steady stream that didn't reach the front door anymore.

She was already daydreaming about the relaxed evening she had planned that would involve a pint of ice cream and a cheesy rom-com, when the chime of the bell at the door alerted her to the next customer. She quickly wound her way to the front, making a mental note that table eleven had been cleared, as long as the new party comprised no more than four people.

As she came around from the back half of the restaurant, she saw who was waiting and ran into a chair. The seated customer jumped, spilling orange juice across the table.

"Oh, I'm so sorry. Let me get you something to clean that up. I'll bring you another juice too. I'm so sorry."

"No, don't worry about it," the woman said, dabbing at the spill with a pile of napkins.

"Nancy." Emily called to another waitress, who was bringing out a fresh stack of pancakes for a lanky gentleman at a nearby table. "I've made a mess here. Would you mind getting her another orange juice and drying this up? I'll look after the customer at the door."

"Yeah, sure. No problem."

Emily straightened her back and approached Liam, who had an amused but friendly smile on his face.

She tried to ignore it. "Hello, Liam. Welcome to Maple Leaf."

"Nice place you've got here. I've heard a lot of good things about it. Lots of great reviews."

"We like it. What are you doing here?" She thought

she was rid of him, but he obviously wasn't done playing his games.

"I thought that would be obvious."

"Well, it's not."

"I'm kinda hungry."

"Oh." Now she felt like an idiot. Of course he was there to eat. Why else would he be there? She had to consider the fact that she was overreacting because she was cut up about losing the house. If she wasn't careful, she'd end up making a fool out of herself.

"This way."

She plastered a wide smile on her face and even pulled the chair out for him. Once he was seated, she handed him the menu. "Can I get you anything to drink?"

"Yeah, a coffee, black."

"Right." She jotted the order on her pad and went to get the drink.

Liam watched her expertly tuck herself through the crowd of tables and exit the dining room. He had his work cut out for him, but he'd had tougher cases.

When she returned with his coffee, he dropped the menu on the table. "So, what's good here?"

"Most people order the All-You-Can-Eat."

"Then I'll have that."

"Plain, buckwheat, wholemeal, or gluten-free?"

"Wow. I didn't know pancakes had so much variety. Um. What would you recommend?"

"Buckwheat."

"Sounds good."

"Did you want anything else with that? Eggs or bacon?"

"No, thanks. The pancakes will be plenty. I hope you don't hold it against me."

She blinked at him. "What?"

"The house. I know it means a lot to you and even though I do own it, it must feel like I'm an intruder."

"No, not at all. It's your house. You're allowed to live there."

"You're welcome anytime."

"Right. Okay." She swiped up his menu without another word and hurried out.

Liam linked his fingers and rested his elbows on the table. Judging by the blush that had appeared at her neck at his invitation, he was sure she was attracted to him. She may not like him, but they had chemistry. As much for him as for her. He wouldn't lie to himself that he wasn't enjoying this. It happened now and then. But attraction meant nothing and could be easily contained. Beautiful women were in abundance, and Emily was simply one more. All he had to do was keep his heart out of it. He had enough on the line as it was.

Emily was flustered when she went to retrieve his order. For reasons she refused to explore, his presence was unnerving. If he intended to stick around for a while, she wouldn't be able to completely avoid him, so she made sure to keep eye contact every time she brought out another plate and made it her mission to appear unfazed.

"The reviews were right," Liam said when he waved away the offer of more. "Maple Leaf deserves its reputation as a must visit in the area. I never eat that much."

"You're not the first person to say that." Her smile this time was genuine. Her dad had worked hard to make the restaurant something special. Having to deal with her mom while he did it was no small feat.

"So, is there anything else I can get you?"

"I don't think I could fit one more thing."

Emily dropped the bill on the table and waited as Liam pulled out his wallet.

When he handed her a fifty, he didn't let go of it when she grabbed it. "Hey, you don't have a minute by any chance?" He knew she didn't, but it was the soft entrance he wanted here, not an affirmative answer. Not yet.

"No, actually I don't. As you can see, we're pretty busy. You going to let go of the money? Or should I come back later?"

He let go of the note. "What time do you get off?"

Her stomach knotted. "I'm here all afternoon. If you'll excuse me, I'll get your change."

She had to remind herself to breathe when she walked away. She couldn't believe he would ask her out on a date, not after everything that had happened. But that's exactly what it sounded like. She paused by the register, frustrated by the warmth it gave her at the thought of a good-looking guy asking her out. She never expected to feel that again. Besides that, Liam was definitely not her type. Definitely. Not. She repeated that a few times before returning to Liam.

"Thank you for visiting with us. I hope you come back soon," she said, laying his change on the table even though he held out his hand for it.

"Do you?" His eyes narrowed.

"Sure."

"It's not a date I'm looking for, if that's what you're worried about."

"Who said I was worried?"

"The wide-eyed look of a deer in the headlights kind of gave it away."

"Oh. It's got nothing to do with you. I'm just … picky." Of all the words she could have chosen. She was hopeless.

"All I want is the chance to apologize," he said. "You caught me off guard. And because you hit me with that shovel, I got defensive. I'm not used to being attacked by beautiful women."

Emily bristled. "Are you trying to be charming? 'Cause if you are, I think you should know, you're better at cocky." She was only half serious but was pleased with the comeback and it showed.

What she didn't know was he'd been waiting for that. A girl like Emily needed to feel like she was on the front foot. He flashed the same million dollar smile again. It failed him the first time, but this time he could see her soften.

"Sorry. Girls in the city like it to be laid on thick. You're obviously not like that, so I apologize. But I really would like to make reparations."

She sucked her bottom lip into her mouth and bit it. "It's really not necessary. And I am genuinely busy. So, have a nice day and good luck with the house."

Man, she was tough to break, but he was too close to back down now. He'd have to use her mother as leverage. He would have preferred to avoid it after the heartache Stevie said she'd been through, but he had no choice. "I really wish you'd reconsider. It's very important to me."

"I find that hard to believe."

Mother was an alcoholic. "See, I'm on this twelve-step program with AA, and I don't want to leave this hanging over my head."

"Oh."

He watched her shoulders drop and knew he had her. He hated himself for it, but it was just a job, not personal. "Yeah."

"How long have you been sober?"

"Twelve months. I'm doing well, but I'm ashamed of how I reacted at the house. Please. If you're busy today, how about tomorrow?"

"Tomorrow I have church."

"Church?" *Why does everyone go to church all of a sudden?*

"Yeah."

"All day?"

She sighed. "Okay, how about lunch?"

"Great. And thank you."

He should have been strutting his way to the parking lot. But instead of the arrogance he usually carried after a job well done, the truth of who he was descended upon him. He wasn't clever; he was just a good liar. That was all. And it wasn't something to be proud of. There was nothing impressive about it.

If the situation had been different, if Sophie weren't involved, he may have made a rash decision right then and there to give it all up, but he couldn't. Of all the moments for him to get a blast of conscience, why did it have to be now when he had no choice but to see this thing through?

"Sit up straight. Chin up." Kyle held his phone out in front of him and took a couple of steps back to get Sophie into the frame. "Say hi to your mom and your uncle and tell them the date."

Sophie obeyed.

"That wasn't so hard, was it?" he said as he continued to record. "You don't have to look so scared. We haven't hurt you, have we?"

"No." Sophie said, her bottom lip quivering.

"You've been fed?"

"Yes."

"Has anyone touched you?"

"No."

"Great." He stopped recording and tossed the phone to the guy standing closest. "Make sure my voice gets edited so it's not recognizable, then send it off to Liam."

He sat down on the couch next to Sophie. "Shouldn't be too much longer and you can go home. You're a pretty girl, but I don't like to get involved in family stuff unless I have to. If your uncle brings me what I want, then this will all be over. And if not." Kyle shrugged. "We'll worry about that when the time comes."

He patted the top of her head and left, heading for his office above the nightclub. It was hours until opening, but the vibration from the music was already humming through him and would soon saturate the entire building when the volume was turned up later.

His phone rang and he slid his finger across the screen. "What?"

"That priest is here."

"What priest?"

"That one who used to turn up."

"Father Carl? Get rid of him."

"I tried. He's not listening."

"Then make him listen."

"Yes, sir."

"No, wait. I'll do it. I don't want him thinking he can turn up whenever he wants."

Kyle found Father Carl, a man in his sixties with soft wavy hair, looking through the bottles of liquor across the bar. "Can I get you a drink? Or were you taking stock of my sins?"

"Kyle, it's good to see you. It's been a while."

"So, which is it?"

"You know I have never judged you."

"I thought priests weren't supposed to lie."

An unceasing mask of patience remained on Carl's face. "Thank you for taking the time to see me. I know this must be … unexpected."

"I can't say I'm not surprised, not after last time. I thought you were smart and took the hint."

"I wouldn't have come except you've been on my heart recently, and I wanted to see how you were doing."

"I'm fine."

"I can't help but think you're heading down a path that will only end badly."

"Oh really? And how'd you work that one out? You must have superpowers because the rest of the world thinks I'm a saint."

"I can't help but feel like I failed you. I was too soft on you."

Kyle barked out a laugh. "Too soft. Wouldn't that have been somethin'?"

"After the way your father treated you, I felt you needed a different sort of parental figure in your life. Not one who used you as an ashtray."

"I've known a lot worse men than my dad."

"I'm sorry for that. I wish I could have done more."

"Are you trying to get under my skin? Because I'll warn you, you'll succeed, but not in the way you're hoping."

"Fair enough." He rested his hand on the bar and drummed his fingers.

"Is there something else?"

"Do you see anything of that boy you used to hang around with? What was his name?"

"You seem hell-bent on dredging up my past. I hope you have a good reason."

"So you don't see him anymore?"

"Liam? Sure, I spoke to him recently. Why?"

"I haven't been sleeping. I didn't want to bother you with it. Not after you made it clear you didn't want to see me again, but it won't leave me alone. I need to tell you that I think you're on your last chance to turn things around."

Kyle looked up at the ceiling. "Still trying to save me," he muttered. "And what does Liam have to do with it?"

"You tell me. I just keep thinking about him. Is he involved?"

Kyle took an aggressive step forward. "Involved in what, exactly? Have you been talking to someone?"

Father Carl didn't back down. "Just God."

"Well, you tell God to mind his own business." He leaned in to whisper, "I can promise you that what I'm into now would curl even his toes."

"I won't stop praying for you."

Kyle choked out a laugh. "Oh, Father, you are one sad man who's been wasting his time praying for someone who doesn't exist anymore. I'm not that broken little boy you dragged out of the gutter. That's not me anymore."

"I don't believe that."

"I don't care if you don't believe it, but trust me, I

am way past redemption and I'm not in the mood for this."

"Okay. I've done what I've come to do, so I'll leave you in peace, although I doubt you have any of that."

"Peace isn't really what I'm after in life."

"Isn't it?" He didn't wait for a reply, just left his words hanging in the air and walked out the door.

Kyle returned to his office and slammed the door. He squeezed the bridge of his nose as he dropped into his chair. He should have let Freddy deal with the priest, but the thought of Father Carl dead in a ditch somewhere sent a shiver up his spine.

The priest was a crazy old man who was obviously obsessed with him.

"Sick." He slammed his hand on the desk as the priest's warning buzzed a hole in his brain. There was no way for Father Carl to know anything about what he did. But what difference did it make if he did? It was nothing that Kyle had to worry about. It didn't matter that the priest was the only man Kyle had ever really trusted. He had not been seeking out the man's advice, so he was under no obligation to heed it.

He noticed a tremor in his hand and fisted it before reaching for a small brown bottle. After depositing a white pill into his shaking palm, he tossed it to the back of his throat and washed it down with a swallow of whiskey.

Chapter 11

EMILY SAT in the second to last row of the church in her usual spot next to a family with a new baby and a two-year-old. She didn't know them well, but they were always really friendly and the kids were cute.

The church was made up of locals, others from nearby towns, and vacationers who didn't want to miss their Sunday service. She always thought it was an odd thing to go to church while you were on vacation. Church was always work for her. Even though she knew it was good for her, there was always that resistance she had to battle on a Sunday morning.

At first, the struggle was attending with her mom growing up. Knowing who the woman was behind closed doors made her sick when she had to listen to people gush about the hours she spent volunteering and what a wonderful mother she must be. It was only later that people discovered the truth.

Then there was that one Sunday not long after she'd returned from the city. During worship, waves of grief had overwhelmed her. She never knew if anyone saw her before she escaped out the back of the church, but it was enough to keep her from coming back for a time. But even that couldn't keep her away forever.

From a young age, she'd had a relationship with God that was very personal to her, and while there was a time she'd stepped away from him, she always found her way back. It was worth the struggle, because without him, she would be lost.

She lifted from her thoughts when she felt a pat on her shoulder. Mrs. Carson gave her a smile and then she and Roger made the slow shuffle to the front, Mr. Carson huffing every time Mrs. Carson stopped to give someone a hug.

"Emily." Wendy, the Carson's neighbor who had seen Liam's light that first night, grabbed her arm. "I heard about Richard Hargrave's son. You must be devastated."

"Not at all."

"Really? Wow, you're taking this all really well."

"It's his house, not mine. It's no big deal."

Wendy patted her arm. "You hang in there."

"Thanks. I will."

"Anytime."

Emily pulled out her phone to read the verse of the day and try to get her head clear of annoyance before the band got up. She loved worship and didn't want it ruined by Wendy's well-meaning interference reminding her of the things she'd lost.

And the LORD commanded the fish, and it vomited Jonah onto dry land.
(Jonah 2:10, New International Version)

She grinned. That's what happened when you let artificial intelligence choose your scriptures. Maybe she should find another app.

"What's funny?" asked a familiar man's voice from beside her.

She looked up. "Liam? What are you doing here?"

He settled in beside her. "Going to church, same as you." He was pleased she didn't shrink away from him. This was progress.

"Didn't know you went."

"Sure." He never went to church with Peter, only a small Bible study for a short time, but he wasn't lying to Emily. Not technically. Once, he and Kyle had sneaked into the back of the Catholic church that Kyle had a connection to. They'd only stayed long enough to scoop out some "holy water" as a dare.

"As surprising as it might sound, I'm not completely devoid of faith." That one was meant to be a lie, but perhaps it was closer to wishful thinking.

She only had time to grunt an interested assent before a group of musicians took to the stage, and everyone stood, including Liam. "We're a well-trained bunch."

She elbowed him, then stilled as the music began.

Halfway through the first song, he glanced sideways to sneak a peek at her but couldn't bring himself to look away straightaway as he had intended. She had her eyes closed and the serene look on her face was one he hadn't seen before. It was a feeling he couldn't say he was familiar with.

As the song built to the bridge, a high-pitched wail drew his attention to the back of the room, where a woman waved a ribbon in long arches through the air. The tempo increased as it transitioned into the next song, and her movement adjusted to accommodate. He pressed his lips into a thin line to hide the smile, then he looked around to see if anyone else was catching the show. No one else had noticed, or they were better at ignoring it than he was. He'd seen some pretty crazy things over the years, but this was new for him.

When the song changed again, something shifted in the atmosphere. It was a familiar tune that scrambled for recognition in the dark recesses of his mind, but he couldn't place it. He also couldn't understand the ache that was building inside, but he didn't seem to be the only one affected. The voices doubled, not in volume, but in capacity, as if the population of the room had increased.

He was having trouble catching his breath as the sound reverberated into the marrow of his bones and something he hadn't felt in a long time stirred within him. The last time he'd felt it was with Peter, a long time ago. It wasn't bad, but he couldn't call it good. It made him want to burst into tears and scream at the top of his lungs. If he had that ribbon in his hand, he could wave it as hard as he could and maybe he'd get some relief. He couldn't look at Emily. He was afraid of what he might find there but didn't know what there was to be afraid of.

Beads of sweat formed on his upper lip as he squeezed his hands into tight fists and sat, leaning his elbows on his knees so he could drop his head between his shoulders. He clasped his hands together as if holding on for dear life. If this didn't finish soon, he'd end up looking crazier than Ribbon Lady.

Then the music settled, and the room went quiet except for some murmuring from a few people.

The intensity diminished and Liam knew he had been given a reprieve from falling off a precipice.

His control returned as someone up the front prayed something about laying down pride and setting aside our own ego in order to connect with the King of Kings and Lord of Lords. To Liam, it sounded like a terrible idea. He had no interest in meeting with God.

He remained distracted for the rest of the service, only noticing Emily when she touched his knee to stop it jiggling the entire row. So much for using church to get closer to her.

The thirty minutes dragged on, and he had no idea what the pastor preached about. What he did know was that if it didn't end soon, he'd have to get up and walk out, which could have unfortunate consequences.

When the service finally closed, Liam twisted out of his seat, ducking through a couple of people who had risen before him. He escaped into the restroom, closing himself in a cubicle. If there was any chance of salvaging the morning, he'd need to compose himself before facing Emily.

The first thing he needed to do was rid himself of the emotional attachment he now had for this weird little church. That was easy. Just focus on the faults. The worship leader was too intense. That lady with the ribbon was obviously a lunatic. The pastor was wearing a terrible tie, and whoever had chosen the paint color for the bathroom should be shot.

Next was reason. His response this morning was nothing more than his subconscious responding to the trauma with his family coupled with his visit to Peter. Seeing Peter always opened old wounds that he was determined to keep closed. That's why he avoided a man he considered to be a friend. Without that visit to Peter, his attendance here this morning would have been a breeze.

And that ego of his that someone had prayed about letting go of in exchange for an encounter with God, he placed that firmly back where it belonged. His confidence quickly surged back, and he was ready for the next round. Nothing would stop him from getting that pendant.

His smile was relaxed when he faced the milling crowd that spilled out the front door.

"Hey there." Someone placed a heavy hand on his shoulder and gave it a squeeze. Liam turned to find a tall, broad man with a crew cut and a friendly smile.

"Hi." Liam held out his hand and the two men assessed each other by a firm shake. Liam wouldn't look Emily's way, but if she caught him having a conversation with a church member, that might soften her even more to him.

"I'm Nathan."

"Liam."

"This your first time?"

"It is. I just came into town."

"Right, excellent. You staying with family?"

"Kind of. My dad was Richard Hargrave. I'm up at his house."

"Right, yeah. Great. How are you finding Oakridge?"

"Oh, I love it. Already making friends."

"Yeah, she sure is a nice town. Moved here thirty years ago and never left."

"Wow, that long." Time to wind it up. "Well, look. It was wonderful to meet you, Nathan. I'm sure I'll see you around." He patted the man on the shoulder and headed toward Emily, who was talking to Ribbon Lady.

He approached slowly, noticing the tight smile and quick glance at the watch, followed by a check of the room.

Perfect timing. She'd had enough of the conversation, and it was time for him to step in and save the day.

"Emily." His grin was wide and appeared genuine as he approached. "You ready for lunch?"

"Liam, there you are. I'd like you to meet Betty. Betty, this is Liam, Richard Hargrave's son."

"Oh." The joyful elation on the woman's face was something to behold. She must have thought pretty highly of his father. Whatever lies he told must have been impressive. "It's so wonderful to meet you."

"You knew my father then?"

"No, I never met him, but I saw him around town."

"Oh."

"It has been wonderful to have you worshipping with us this morning. Did you enjoy the service?"

"Yeah. It was somethin' else."

"Wonderful." She leaned forward and gave him a big hug.

"Wonderful," he said into her neck. He caught Emily's eyes and lifted his brows. She smiled, enjoying his discomfort.

"Well." Betty was flustered now. "I've got to get off home. I've got a roast on. You two have a wonderful lunch." She turned for the door but stopped, a frown darkening her face. "Liam."

"Yes, Betty?"

"God wants you to know that he saw you this morning."

His stomach hit the floor. "Uh."

"I mean, he really saw you. He was here. You felt that, didn't you? I can see it on your face. He wants you to know that you don't have to be afraid."

Liam swallowed hard. "Thanks, Betty. Now, you better hurry. You've got that roast."

"Right you are. Thanks, Liam. Hope to see you next Sunday."

Liam waved her off, feeling completely unsettled. "So … she's crazy."

"By the way your face paled, I'd have to disagree."

"And you're enjoying my discomfort, aren't you?"

"I must admit, I am. But seriously, are you okay?"

"Why wouldn't I be? God saw me, remember? I must be doing something right." Liam directed Emily toward the door. "But what I really find fascinating is that she's never met my father, yet she greets me like I'm the son of a king?"

"She greets everyone like that."

"Why?"

"Because she believes everyone *is* a son of the king."

"Richard Hargrave is anything but a king."

"That's not who I was referring to."

"Oh, you mean King of Kings and all that? Wow, that's intense."

"Betty might be extreme, but she doesn't pretend to be anyone other than who she is. Ribbons and all."

"You know, I've only heard a legend of the infamous ribbon dances that take place at some churches, but I've never seen one in person until now."

"Yes, the dance is … special."

"If you're not careful, she may single-handedly empty the place out."

"What a horrible thing to say."

"You don't agree?"

"No. No one else minds besides you."

"I doubt that's true."

"Fine, but *I* certainly don't mind. She's different, sure, but I find that refreshing. She's not afraid to be honest about who she is. If we can't handle that, that's our problem, not hers. You know, you're not the first person she's given an encouraging word to either."

"That was supposed to be encouraging?"

"Wasn't it?"

"I found it alarming."

"Maybe that's what you need. That woman knows her Bible inside and out. More often than not, when she rattles off a scripture or something like what she said to you, the person ends up sobbing on her shoulder. People aren't afraid to be vulnerable with her because she's already pushed the boundaries of normal. She may be the only person I know who I can be confident won't judge me."

"Okay, so she's a nice person, but you can't say she's never scared anyone away. 'Cause I was probably close."

"Maybe that's good. Maybe we don't want your type around here."

"Ouch. That's harsh."

"As harsh as telling Betty she can't worship at the back of the church out of everyone's way because ribbon dances aren't what us civilized people consider 'normal'?" She paused to make sure he got her point. "We take people as they are here, and if you're not willing to do the same … " She shrugged in challenge.

Liam started laughing.

"Why is that funny?"

"It's not funny like that. It's brilliant, what you said. I am now a ribbon dance convert." He wasn't lying. He loved her passion and was having trouble hiding the fact.

"Are you picking on me?"

"No. I'm not as horrible as you might think. Yes, I was a bit put off by Betty, but I actually agree with you." It was probably one of the only completely truthful things he'd said to her. He needed to stay away from truthful. It was too dangerous. "We learn a lot about that in AA."

"Yeah, I guess you would. The last thing you need is people judging you. That's why I think the church should be an environment where people can come in and not be afraid to be honest about who they are."

"You feel like you can do that here?"

"I wouldn't say I'm there yet, but I'm headed in that direction. People will always make mistakes, and churches are full of people, so … "

"So you're not?"

"Not what?"

"Honest about who you are?"

"Are you?"

"Should we get some lunch?"

Emily laughed. "Yes, I'm starving."

"You want to take my bike?"

"She's a nice-looking bike, but no. I'll drive myself." Liam was sure that would have gotten her. Maybe next time. "There's a café down by the lake that serves fantastic open grilled sandwiches."

"Sounds good. I'll follow you there."

Chapter 12

THE SUN WARMED the seats on the deck enough to sit outside and enjoy the view.

"I love sitting out here. I'm glad we've finally reached the turning point in the season," Emily said, squinting up at the sun. "Must have been beautiful looking out over the lake this morning."

"It was. Is that what you do? Is that the deal with that house? You go there and enjoy the views?"

Emily stabbed at her ice cubes with the straw. "Yeah. It's been a kind of refuge for me."

"Did you go up there when my dad was there?"

"Your dad invited me over for a cup of coffee one day, and I kind of never left."

"Oh." He made a face.

"No, it wasn't like that. Gross. No. He was older than my dad. He said he wanted someone to enjoy the view since he didn't think he deserved it."

"Sounds like a line."

"Maybe it was, but I didn't get that vibe from him. It all started when we got to talking one day at the restaurant. He always looked sad, so I tried to cheer him up by telling him how much I admired his house and would daydream about the furniture I would fill it with."

"It could certainly use something decent. My dad didn't fill it with much worth keeping."

She squinted at him. "Well, there is a bureau up there that I gave to him. I thought he could use something special to look at every day."

"Wait, you made that dresser?"

"Yeah."

"That is a beautiful piece."

"I thought you said there was nothing worth keeping."

"No, I said there wasn't much. I can't believe you made that. I've been admiring it since I arrived."

"It's not that exciting."

"I don't agree. I've done some work with antiques and I can tell you that is something special."

"You work in the antiques business?"

Liam's jaw twitched. "Yeah, kind of."

"Buying and selling, or collecting?"

He cleared his throat. "Buying and selling." Time to put the subject back on her. "You could make a lot of money."

Emily shrugged. "It's not what I want to spend my time doing."

"Wait, you'd rather waitress than make good money doing something that you are obviously gifted in?"

"I don't normally waitress. I'm helping my dad."

"Surely your dad recognizes your talent. You are wasted working at a restaurant."

She pinched her lips together and leaned back to make room when their orders were brought out. She dug in so she could stop talking.

He watched her take a big bite. "So that's it? You just stopped?"

"Stopped what?" she said out of the side of her mouth.

"Making furniture."

"I still make some."

"Great. Where do you sell it? I might buy a piece."

She shrugged again and took another bite.

"You don't sell it? So you make high end furniture and give it away."

"To people who deserve it. Mr. and Mrs. Carson now have a set of beautiful bedside tables that they could never have afforded."

"That's really nice, but you can give away furniture to some and sell it to those who can afford it. So what happened?"

"What makes you think something happened?"

"I saw that look on your face."

She set her fork down on her plate. "What look?"

Liam put his hands up in surrender. "It's okay, you don't have to tell me."

"I had a bad experience in New York."

"Bad how?"

"I got mixed up in the wrong crowd."

"And that is a good enough reason to stop using your

talent?" Liam saw the haunted look Stevie had mentioned and knew he'd pushed it too far. It also unnerved him that he had a desire to put a protective arm around her. "Sorry. That was unfair." He took a bite of his lunch. "This is superb." He saw her exhale in relief at the change in subject.

"Yeah. I love this place."

He made a choice to spend the rest of the lunch helping her forget her troubles by telling stories of some of the adventures he'd had. It started out as a way to get her to trust him, but every time she laughed, he searched for more details he could share that would bring back that sound. At one point, they were both in tears.

For the next hour, the job faded into the background, along with the guard he was supposed to keep up. By the time they wound things up, the sun was dipping low and it was hard to say goodbye. He wanted to spend more time getting to know her and lied to himself that it was all for the pendant.

"I enjoyed that," he said, leaning his arm on the tailgate of her truck.

"Unfortunately, yes, it was fun."

"Unfortunately? Ouch. Man, what's a guy gotta do around here?"

"When I agreed to have lunch with you, I still thought you were one of those conniving, arrogant bad boys who all the girls stupidly fell for and then their lives get ruined forever."

"I hope you don't mind, but I'm going to take that as a compliment."

"I wouldn't if I were you. I was one of those girls once. It wasn't pretty."

"You? Really?" He desperately wanted to know more but was afraid to ask. Afraid of how it would make him feel toward her. He had to keep that protective response buried deep because in the end, it was Liam who would be the one to hurt her. He had gotten side-tracked during lunch and needed to refocus. You had to leave them wanting more.

"I guess I'll see you around," he said.

"Oh? So you're planning on sticking around town then?"

"Don't know. We'll see."

"Well, listen. I'd really like to put our first meeting behind us."

"That sounds good."

"I'd like to at least think we can be friends. Every now and then, I really need a good laugh."

"Don't we all?"

"Can I ask you a personal question? You don't have to answer, but — "

"Go ahead."

"Why'd you come back now?"

He took a minute to process the question. "It was time."

"I know you didn't have a great relationship with your dad. He told me. But I thought you should know that he regretted it. He told me he had messed up and wished he could make it right." His eyes shifted to the ground. "I'm sorry. I don't mean to upset you."

"No, it's okay. He tried to get in touch with me, but I couldn't do it. By then, it was too late. He'd made his bed."

"Okay, well, I wanted you to know that he was sorry."

"I should get going."

"Look, I'm really sorry if I said the wrong thing."

"No, it's fine. You've done nothing wrong. You've been great. I've just got to get going. I'll see you around."

Liam walked up the steps to his porch with a cloud hanging over his head. He didn't owe his dad anything, but it didn't make sense how a dead man could still cause such a sharp pain deep in his guts.

His phone vibrated in his coat pocket. "Kyle, what a pleasant surprise."

"I want my pendant, Liam."

Liam waited until he stood at the edge of the porch, looking out over the lake, before he responded. "I told you I'd get it."

"You used to be someone I could count on."

"Someone you could count on to get into trouble with."

"Yeah, whatever happened to that kid?"

"The trouble you started getting into was not to my taste."

"You never could stomach the stuff with the biggest payoff."

"Too rich for my taste."

"Well, getting your hands on a little pendant shouldn't be too difficult."

"I need more time."

"I'm afraid if I give you too much rope, you'll hang yourself."

"Kyle, you know how these things can work. If I push too hard, I'll miss my chance. Let me do what I'm best at."

"Is she pretty?"

"Who?"

"The mark."

"It's not a woman."

"You sure?"

"I think I can tell if someone is a woman."

"Fine. You can have a little more time, but I want you to understand, Liam, that once our little deal is settled, I want nothing more to do with you. Do you understand? No more surprises from you. You stay out of my business, or I'll kill you myself. I never want to see you again."

"I'm happy with that arrangement."

"Good." Kyle hung up.

Liam put a hand across his throat. It wasn't Kyle who gave him the rope to hang himself. He was doing that all on his own. If he didn't get control of this connection he had to Emily, he'd make a mess of everything.

It was foolish to allow himself to feel anything for

her. Even without Sophie's life on the line, they could never be together. They were from two different worlds. It was only a romantic notion written about in fairy tales that meant someone like Liam could ever be with someone like Emily. They were not destined for anything other than pain and regret.

He sent her a text and went inside.

Chapter 13

EMILY COLLAPSED ONTO HER COUCH, her arms laying limply at her side. She had not expected, or wanted, to have such a good time with Liam. It was supposed to be lunch. That was all. He was supposed to apologize, and she'd accept, and then they'd go their separate ways.

Thank goodness for the constant companion of her niggling anxiety that kept her grounded. Her growing attraction to Liam and the thrill of spending time with someone who made her feel light-headed was nothing more than a nice distraction. It gave her a break from her fear but wasn't a reason to abandon all sensibility. She wasn't in a position to open herself up to anyone, especially a stranger.

She jumped when she heard a knock at the door. "Is that you, Dad?"

"No, it's Stacey."

"You have impeccable timing. Come in."

Stacey tucked her head through the door and

assessed her friend, who now had a distraught arm draped across her forehead.

They had been a year apart in high school and only knew each other by sight, but when Emily returned from the city, they met at church and became good friends quickly. Stacey knew Emily well these days, but she didn't know everything.

"Hey," Stacey said.

"Hey. I thought you were working today."

"I finished early." She joined her friend on the couch.

"Nice. You want to watch a movie or something? I could use a distraction."

"From what I hear, you already have one."

Emily's groan was exaggerated but she meant every last rumble. "This town. What did you hear?"

"Word is you had a date with the hot new guy in town. That is so unlike you."

"It wasn't a date."

"What was it then?"

"Lunch."

"A minor detail. What about the other one?"

"Other what?"

"Detail. Is he hot?"

"He's not bad looking."

"Meaning … "

"You'd probably call him hot."

"I can't believe this. They're also saying he came to church with you."

"He didn't come *with* me. He turned up on his own."

"Man, I'm so bummed I had to work this morning and missed it. Does he really ride a motorcycle?"

"Yes."

"Did he take you for a ride?"

"He offered."

"Don't tell me you said no."

"Of course I did."

"And?"

"And what?"

Stacey tsked and threw herself back on the couch. "Why are you being evasive? This must be serious."

"No, it's not serious. It's definitely not serious. Serious is the last thing it is."

"Wow, so it is." Stacey raked her fingers through her short hair, making it poke out in different directions.

"No. We don't even know each other. He's recently turned up in town. He's actually Richard Hargrave's son."

"Hargrave … why do I know that name?"

"He owned that house on top of the hill. Left it to his son."

"Whoa, wait. You're saying that this guy owns the house you love?"

"Yeah."

"Emily, this is your happily-ever-after. Marry this guy for his house if you have to."

"You're joking."

Stacey offered a wry grin instead of responding.

"You're terrible."

"Of course I'm joking, but still. It's worth at least giving it a chance."

"Why is it that married people are always trying to get their friends into relationships? Are you that unhappy in your marriage that you're trying to live vicariously through me? 'Cause I thought Tony was a good guy, and I can promise you I'll disappoint you, big-time."

Stacey squawked out a laugh. "I love Tony, but after five years of marriage it's not often that I get all shivery at the sight of him."

"Can you still get shivery at the sight of him?"

"I saw him doing chin-ups the other day. That was pretty hot."

Emily laughed. "Can Tony do chin-ups?"

"Probably not a lot, but he only needed to do one."

"That's adorable."

"Exactly. I want that for you. Can this guy do chin-ups?"

Emily couldn't help the flush that heated her face. "Uh, yeah, he's pretty fit."

"Ooh. Well, there you go."

"You want me to fall in love with a guy because he's fit?"

"No, what I want is for you to be happy."

"I am happy."

"Are you, though?"

"A guy isn't going to fix my baggage."

"At least you're willing to admit you've got it."

"I never denied it."

"But you won't open up about it."

"There's nothing to tell."

"Fine, don't tell me. I've gotta get going anyway. I

just wanted to hear firsthand what all the fuss was about."

"Like most small-town gossip, it's been blown way out of proportion. There's nothing going on and there will be nothing going on."

"Whatever you say. Just make sure I'm the first to know if anything changes."

"The way this town gossips, I can't promise you you'll be the first to hear scandal, but you'll be the first to know the truth."

As soon as Stacey left, a text came through from Liam asking when he could see her again.

She set the phone on the table in front of her while she figure out how to respond. Her heart was screaming yes. Or maybe that was the butterflies in her stomach. But butterflies were untrustworthy. They could flap their wings and change the course of humanity and she couldn't risk it. This was a matter for her head to work out.

She typed out three different versions of the same message before settling on: *Sorry, got a lot on this week. Maybe some other time.*

A little passive-aggressive, maybe, but she hoped he understood that "some other time" meant never.

After tossing her phone aside, she picked up her Bible, staring at the front cover. It was possible she'd spend the rest of her life alone. How do you get past something you can barely remember but that causes terror to grip so tightly you still feel like you might die?

A metal basket hung off Liam's forearm as he strolled the aisles of the small grocery store. Emily's brush-off was unexpected and hurt more than as simply being a glitch in his plans. Whatever wounds she carried went deeper than he realized, and he was about to add to them. The only way he could keep moving forward was by picturing Sophie and allowing the rage to kindle a fire that burned away any feelings he had developed.

He rounded into the pasta aisle and recognized the old lady at the other end. She was reaching for an item on the top shelf. Liam hurried to help.

"Let me get that for you."

She turned to him, a look of curiosity preceding a gummy grin. "Why, thank you, young man."

"Is this the one?" He pulled a jar of spaghetti sauce down.

"Oh my, no. Did you see the price? I'm after the one on sale. They put those the highest so you can't see them."

"Clever trick. I'll keep that in mind." He handed her the cheaper jar. "Hey, don't I know you from somewhere?"

"I don't know why you should, but I know you."

"You do?"

"You're the gentleman who recently came into town and had lunch with Emily."

"News travels fast."

"We look after one another around here."

"But I do know you. Or at least I recognize you. From church yesterday. That's where I saw you."

"Were you there?"

"I was. I hate to miss a Sunday."

Her mouth puckered into an impressed *O*. "That's nice to hear. Too many young ones these days have thrown away their faith in exchange for unworthy things."

"I agree. It's sad, really. I sat with Emily, but I saw you up front."

"Emily is a lovely girl."

"Yes. She's been very kind to me since I've been in town. Actually, maybe you could help me."

"I'd be happy to, if I can."

"I'd like to get Emily a gift to say thank you for her kindness. Do you know her well enough to know what I could get?"

"Yes! I've known Emily since she was born. Watched her grow up."

"It's a good thing I stopped to help you, then."

"Ooh, must be a God appointment."

"A what?"

"God appointment. The pastor spoke about that earlier in the year. About how God is involved in our everyday lives and brings about certain circumstances for good."

Liam frowned. What he had planned was definitely not connected to a God appointment. It might help things work out for him and his family, but it would not be pleasant for Emily. Betrayal never was. "Then this is definitely a God appointment."

Her eyes squinted with the smile. "Now let me think. You'll want to get her something thoughtful, but not too extravagant. She's not that kind of girl."

"No, I didn't think she was."

"Ah! I know just the thing. Driftwood."

"Hmm. It certainly isn't extravagant. Are you sure?"

"Not extravagant, but very thoughtful. She used to be obsessed with driftwood. She'd walk miles around the lake collecting it. Made some beautiful pieces with it, as I recall, although I haven't seen any in a while. Maybe you could find some nice bits for her to work with again. I don't know if that's helpful."

"That's brilliant."

"Wonderful. I'm glad I could help."

"I'm sorry, what was your name?"

"Mrs. Carson."

"Well, Mrs. Carson, you've been amazing. I can't wait to see the look on her face."

She clapped her hands. "And it's a lovely day today too. Perfect day for a walk if you wanted to."

"I'm going to do that. I can't wait to give it to her."

Liam slipped into the next aisle, grabbing the couple of things he needed for himself and then headed for the register. The driftwood was perfect. Maybe it was a God appointment after all. If God existed, he must care about Sophie's life, but how to reconcile that with hurting Emily …

He stopped short when he saw a guy, obviously strung out on drugs, looking through magazines near the front door. Liam had spent enough time in the shadows with the broken to know when something shady was going on. It could have been the twitching, or the eyes that kept lifting to scan the room, but whatever it was, Liam's muscles were straining in anticipation of the man's next move, whatever it might be.

He stayed back out of the guy's line of sight and lowered his basket to the floor. Even though he'd rather avoid getting involved, he couldn't make it out the door before the action started. He was in this whether he liked it or not.

Liam continued to watch as the man put down the magazine and reached a hand into his pocket. It bumped around, grappling with something.

The front door slid open and another customer entered, passing by the soon-to-be assailant. Both Liam and the man looked at the newcomer.

While Liam's breath caught in his throat, the man moved into action, jerking a knife out of his pocket and lunging for Emily, who had just walked in. He swung around behind her with the knife pushed into her throat.

"Everybody freeze or I'll kill her."

It took several terrifying seconds before those close by understood what had happened. After a few gasps and one scream, the other patrons settled into a stunned silence.

"I want your money. Hand it over or I'll kill her." His voice was ragged and choked but still loud enough to be menacing. He dragged Emily around so he could block off the door or threaten anyone else who was unlucky enough to walk in. "I said, I'll kill 'er."

Emily couldn't stop the swallow of fear that pressed her throat into the tip of the knife, and she was sure it drew blood. Pins and needles spread over her body and her vision blurred as panic spread through her. She knew this guy from around town. He'd been in and out of drug rehab, or so the gossip went, and had come home recently to be looked after by his grandmother. She knew Margaret enough to have gotten the real story. He never made it to rehab and only turned up when he wanted something. Margaret had to hide her money, but he'd still take anything she had of value and pawn it. Emily had considered taking the information to the police, but Margaret begged her not to, so Emily tried to be a comforting ear, instead. Now she was paying for her inaction.

She looked around for help, but no one would make eye contact. They were either focused on the knife, the attacker, or the floor. Most people had their hands raised, but only a few were pulling out money, hesitating while they waited to see what the others would do.

"Come on!" Spit flew out of his mouth and caught her cheek. "Hand it over."

Emily whimpered. It couldn't end this way, not after everything, not when she thought she could hide from the world in her little town and be safe. The edges of her vision dimmed until she saw Liam step out into the open.

"Hey, man," he said, taking a few steps forward with his hands raised. "We're going to help you out here. I'm going to get my wallet, okay? But can you do me a favor and give that knife a little space? You've already drawn some blood and you don't want to lose your captive, right?"

The guy jerked and angled the knife more directly into her throat. "Give me your wallet."

"Yeah, sure." He looked Emily in the eye as a small, reassuring smile played on his lips before he focused on the knife. She swallowed, then winced as her throat pressed against the tip again.

Liam licked his bottom lip as he inched closer. It would have been better to have a space between knife and skin, but he'd have to go with it. This guy would likely slice her throat without even meaning to the way he twitched.

He leaned forward when he got close and tossed his wallet at the man's feet. When the assailant's attention focused on the floor, Liam leaped forward, clamping his hand on the druggie's knife wrist, yanking it toward him. He swung the guy around so he lost his grip on Emily, who squealed as she went flying sideways into a display after a helpful shove from Liam.

After twisting the guy's arm around his back and sending the knife skidding across the floor, Liam fell on top of him, knocking the wind out of the now helpless man.

"Someone want to call the cops?" Liam said as he scouted the room for someone suitable to take his place.

A woman stepped forward. "I, yeah, I did."

"Good." Liam spotted a big guy in his fifties who looked like he knew how to handle himself. He nodded to him. "Can you give me a hand here?" The man hurried forward. "What's your name?"

"Keith."

"Keith, would you mind holding him down for me?"

"Uh, yeah, sure." The man got awkwardly on his knees, but then didn't hesitate to lean his full weight to keep the guy in place.

Liam jumped up and rushed to Emily, who was still on the ground in a pile of snack boxes, one arm wrapped around her middle and the other at her throat. She stared at nothing.

"Hey," he said, trying to get her attention. When he spoke, her eyes slowly moved to focus on him. "You okay?"

She pressed her lips together and tears brimmed in her eyes but didn't fall.

"Come here." He put an arm around her to help her up. "Hey, Keith," he said, half carrying Emily toward the door. "I'm going to take Emily home, so can you tell the police they can find us there when they want to get a statement?"

"Yeah, sure. No problem at all. She gonna be okay?"

"Yeah, just a bit of shock, that's all. But it'll be better for her to recover at home."

Chapter 14

WHEN LIAM PULLED into the driveway, he was glad to see Emily's dad sitting on the porch. He didn't want to be seen taking her into her house alone. Not the way this town talked. He might relieve her of the necklace, but he could be honorable in some things.

Liam waved through the windshield and watched as Emily's father lifted a hand to wave back but stopped when he realized Emily wasn't the driver.

"What's your dad's name?" he asked Emily, who had been silent on the short drive home.

"Huh?"

"Your dad. What's his name?"

"Sam."

Liam got out of the truck and waved again. "Hi, Sam. There was an incident at the grocery store, but Emily's okay."

Sam was already walking down the steps, but now ran for the truck, a slight limp becoming prominent in his haste. When he reached Emily's door, he yanked it open.

"Sweetheart? Are you okay?"

She blinked back her tears at the sound of his voice, but couldn't look at him, not without falling apart.

Sam reached across his daughter and unbuckled her, carefully unwrapping her arm from the strap.

She took a few deep breaths to get control. "Thanks, Dad." He'd be worried and she couldn't let him worry. "I'm okay,"

He put his arm around her shoulders to help her out.

"I'm okay, really. I can do it."

Liam stood back and watched, waiting to see if his help was needed. He wasn't convinced yet that she wouldn't pass out because of the shock.

She steadied herself before allowing her dad to lead her to the house.

"I think I need some fresh air," she said when they reached the front door.

Liam held the porch swing steady as she lowered herself into it.

"Do you mind if I run inside and get her a glass of water?" Liam said quietly to Sam. "You should probably sit with her for a minute."

"Yeah, sure. Thanks."

Liam rummaged through the cupboards until he found a glass. There was a short time in his life when helping people was what he did. Not stealing and deceiving. It's what Peter had trained him for. But that all changed on his last mission.

He'd never forget the broken body of that little boy who'd looked up at him with his big dark eyes and mumbled through a gargle of blood. The words the boy spoke were probably in Arabic, but to Liam it sounded like he had said, "sorry" over and over again. The same painful word Liam repeated in his own head.

Cold water spilling over his hand brought him back to himself and he turned off the tap.

He stopped at the living room when he went past and saw pictures of Emily and her dad on the fireplace mantle. He looked at the drawers he could go through right now, undetected while Emily and Sam were distracted outside. There were magazines that would give him insight into Sam, all of which would give him more leverage.

He looked down at the glass in his hand and headed for the front door.

Sam sat close to his daughter. He was afraid she'd close herself off again like she had before.

"So I take it that was the guy you had lunch with on Sunday?"

Emily pinched the bridge of her nose. "I'm sorry you had to hear about it that way."

"Three different people were very excited to tell me all about it. I pretended I already knew and was quite adamant that it was no big deal."

"Thank you."

"So, can you tell me what happened today?"

"It was nothing."

"Don't tell me that. I know you're shaken up. If you don't want to tell me, you know I'll still be here for you, but … "

He was never one to push her for information, and she'd never offered before, but today was different. Today was something she could share with him. She owed him that.

"You know that young guy who came back to stay with his grandmother, Margaret?"

"Yeah, the one who's been in rehab."

She sighed. "I don't think he ever went to rehab. He tried to hold up the store and get some money."

"That wasn't a very smart plan. Most people in town would know either who he is or where he's staying."

"He was pretty high. He couldn't have been thinking beyond getting money for his next hit."

"Poor Margaret. She's going to be horrified when she finds out."

"Or maybe she'll be relieved. I think he was taking advantage of her. Him being in jail will keep her safe."

He shook his head. "Did he threaten you? You still look pretty pale."

Emily bit her lip. "Just remember I'm okay."

"Oh, dear."

"I don't want you to get upset, but he grabbed me. Held a knife to my throat."

"Emily."

"Liam saved me. Jumped on the guy and took him down."

"Who did what?" Liam asked as he came out the door.

Sam stood and hugged him. Liam almost dropped the water. "What's this about?" He looked over Sam's shoulder to Emily, who was smiling. It was nice to see.

"You saved my girl. What can I ever do to repay you?"

"You don't have to do anything." Liam extracted himself and handed Emily the water, then leaned against a post. "I did what was necessary at the time."

"But how'd you do it?" Sam asked.

"I grabbed his arm, yanked him ar — "

"No, I mean, how do you know how to do that stuff? He had a knife, right? I don't know many people who would be able to, let alone know how, to disable an armed man and subdue him."

"I've had some training. A long time ago. I don't normally do stuff like that anymore."

"I'm glad you made an exception today."

"I couldn't stand around while someone got hurt. Not when I could help." He didn't like the attention on him. "Emily, your color's looking better. I can probably leave you two to your evening."

"No, please stay. Please. I've got a casserole in the oven. There's plenty to go around. I'd love it if you stayed for dinner. It's the least I can do."

Liam looked at Emily, who gave him a small nod. "If it's as good as your pancakes, I guess I'll have to stay."

"Have you been to the restaurant?"

"I have. Great place."

Sam clapped his hands together. "Great. I'll cut up a few extra potatoes."

After he went inside, Liam moved around to sit beside Emily. "How are you feeling?"

"A little shaky." She focused on her fingers. "What you said about not standing by when you could help?"

"Yeah."

"I knew that guy. The druggie. Not personally, but I knew he was taking advantage of his grandmother. I never reported him. If I had, none of this would have happened."

Liam dug his feet into the floor, swinging the seat. "Don't do that to yourself. There have been plenty of times in my life where I chose wrong. Making mistakes is part of life. You learn from them and move forward."

"That's a very grown-up thing to say."

"I've got a few gems tucked away. I don't always live by them, but they're handy to pass on."

"One thing's for sure. If I ever know about something going on that's not right, I won't ignore it. Margaret didn't want to me to say anything, and I was stupid for doing what she asked. She was trying to protect her grandson, but that's not what it did. I can't afford to stay silent. Not when people are in trouble."

"You don't always stay silent, you know. You didn't stay silent with that politician, and you definitely weren't silent when you found me at the house."

"That was different. No one was there to tell me not to make a fuss. So from now on, I'll always make a fuss."

"I don't think you can blanket it like that. Sometimes keeping quiet is the right thing to do."

"The things that have kept me quiet over the years are the things that have hurt me the most." She anchored her feet to stop the swing. "Do you think he would have killed me if you weren't there?"

"I'm not comfortable answering that question."

"So that's a yes, then?"

"Try not to think about what-ifs."

"When you stepped out, when I saw you, I knew. Somehow, I knew it would be okay. Even though I didn't know you could do all of that."

"What do you mean you didn't know? Have you already forgotten how I handled myself when you hit me with the shovel? I'm a well-oiled machine."

"Oh, great. You're going to bring that up again? I was trying to forget." She laughed. "I must have looked like such an idiot."

"No, you were good. Very impressive."

"Liar."

"Okay, fine. I didn't feel very threatened. But it was a good effort."

"Were you in the army or something? Is that where you were trained?"

"I was part of a special forces team years ago."

"And you still remember all the training?"

"They really drill it in to you."

"So I guess you can do a few chin-ups?" She bit back on her smile. Stacey would be impressed.

"I can do a few, yeah." He looked up at the rafter

and had a strong urge to jump up and show her. *What, am I twelve all of a sudden?*

"Lucky for me, you came into town just in time."

That brought him back to reality. He focused out at the road to hide his frown. "Lucky you."

"I might go grab a shower before dinner. You can go in and hang out with my dad if you're brave enough." She lifted her eyebrows as she stood.

"I would love to get grilled by your dad. It would be a pleasure."

He waited until she'd gone into the garage before he went inside. He couldn't believe he was falling for her.

He found Sam humming, a hand towel draped over his shoulder while he chopped potatoes. "Smells good. Anything I can help with?"

"Where's Emily?"

"Shower."

"Good. I hoped to have a chat with you alone." Sam flipped the large knife he had been using into the air and the point stuck in the cutting board.

"Sounds ominous. So, I should be worried?"

"You saved her life, and I give you a lot of extra points for that. But I know nothing else about you."

"What do you want to know?"

"Just that you won't hurt her. She's fragile. I mean, don't get me wrong, she's a tough girl, but she's got stuff she's dealing with. Stuff that even I don't know about. She seems okay, but I want you to know, if you care about her, you'll keep protecting her like you did today."

Liam anchored his hand on the counter for support. "I've got a niece named Sophie. Beautiful kid full of life.

She was in trouble once and I put everything on the line to save her. That's the kind of guy I try to be." He just wouldn't be able to be that guy for Emily.

Sam nodded and went back to his chopping. "It's nice to know you have family you care about. I didn't know your father, but I gather you didn't have a great relationship with him?"

"No."

"But he always did right by Emily."

"She seems like the sort of person a lot of people would do right by."

"There are many people who care about her. Unfortunately, she struggled to get that at home, and I was partly to blame. She had a hard time with her mom. If I'm honest, so did I. But I loved her mom and always stuck up for her, even in her abuse. I made a lot of mistakes, but … I want Emily to be happy."

"I can't promise you she'll be safe forever, but for my part" — the words almost choked him — "I'll never do anything to hurt her."

"Good. That's settled. You any good with a knife?"

"I'm passable."

"Great, you can cut up some carrots."

Chapter 15

AFTER DINNER, the three moved into the living room, and Sam started a fire. "That's better. These nights still give off quite a chill."

"Yeah, sure, Dad." She looked at Liam. "He doesn't stop making fires until he needs air-conditioning. Then he moves it into the backyard."

"I love fires." Liam scooted forward in his seat, holding his hands out even though he was warm enough.

Sam stood. "I might hit the hay. I'm beat. You two stay as long as you like. Just turn off the lights when you're done here."

"Dad, you never go to bed before ten."

"I didn't get a good night's sleep last night."

"Whatever you say." She knew what he was doing but wasn't sure whether or not she was happy about it. "You want a coffee or something?" she asked Liam after her dad left.

"You have any hot chocolate?"

"Really?"

"Yeah, with marshmallows if you've got them."

"I'm not sure. I'll have to check."

Liam joined her in the kitchen as she rooted through the pantry. "Well, what do you know? My dad is a closet hot chocolate drinker. Shouldn't surprise me." She held up a large container. "This one's my favorite too."

"Oh, so you're a hot chocolate drinker yourself?"

"Not since I was a girl, but this kind, with the tiny marshmallows inside, was always my favorite."

"I haven't had hot chocolate in a long time, either, but the fire sort of lends itself to it, I think."

She scooped the chocolate into cups while the water boiled. "So, my dad said he told you about my tremulous relationship with my mom."

"He did. Should he not have?"

"He has a tendency to overshare, but he means well."

"At least we're even now."

"Are we?"

"You already know my relationship with my dad wasn't great."

"True."

With the drinks in hand, they went back to the living room. Liam sat on the couch next to Emily this time. Close enough he could bump her leg with his.

She smiled at him as she took a sip, and he knew he had her. This would be the perfect time to finish the job. He could see the path through to the ending he wanted, but all he could think about was keeping that smile on her face.

He looked into the fire and tried picturing Sophie, but even that didn't work. All it meant was that now he had two people he wanted to protect. Being with Emily and her dad, listening to their stories, knowing the pain Emily carried from her past, but not knowing what it was, it had completely messed with his head. The answer to his problems was no longer clear.

Emily spoke again. "My mom wasn't all bad. She left me some good stuff too."

"Oh yeah?"

"In a roundabout way. She's the reason I know God."

"You're serious?"

"Yeah. She's the one who dragged me along every Sunday to church and that's where I met him."

"God."

"Yeah."

"So the fact that your mom went to church didn't put you off?"

"No. Maybe God gave me grace for that. I never connected the way he is to the way my mom was. Everything I learned in Sunday school and youth group was mine. It wasn't connected to her. I knew deep down that it mattered to God how hard my relationship with my mom was, and that meant a lot to me. I never confused her behavior with God's."

"What about your dad?"

"He's a Christian, but he doesn't go to church. He didn't have the same experience I did. Mom was really hard on him and I think he's ashamed and I hate that. I hate what things like shame do to people."

"But *you're* there every Sunday?"

"Yeah, but that's 'cause I'm trying to do what's best. That doesn't mean that I don't struggle with my relationship with God. I struggle all the time to understand the right way forward in life, and I have no idea why I'm telling you all of this."

"I'm glad you are." He needed to stop. He had to get out of there. This was personal. He couldn't let it be personal. "There was a time I was pretty close to God."

"Yeah?"

"I couldn't handle it. Couldn't reconcile myself to it. With all the turmoil spinning me in circles, in the end it was easier to go my own way."

"That's one thing I've never done. I mean, I've pushed God aside now and then, but I couldn't imagine trying to do life on my own."

"But he hasn't been able to help?"

"Help what?"

"Whatever haunts you."

"You think something haunts me?"

"Is it your mom?"

"If only it were that simple."

"The stuff that follows us from our past never is."

"And what about you?"

"What about me?"

"You're running from something, right?"

"What makes you say that?"

"I don't know. Everything about you says you're running away."

"I'm not running from anything."

"No? What do you do for a living? Where did you come from? If you're not running, then you're hiding."

"I guess we all have our secrets."

"What is it you have against God?" Emily hadn't meant to ask the question out loud.

"What makes you think I have anything against him?"

"Then tell me you don't."

"I told you I was a Christian once."

"Once."

"I don't have anything against God. We just aren't compatible. If you knew the things I've done in my life, you'd understand."

"Isn't that the point, though? That we've all screwed up. Some are worse than others, but we're all a mess in one way or another and Jesus is the only one who can change that."

Liam laughed. "That's basically what Peter said to me."

"Peter?"

"He was my training officer in special forces. He said the same thing you just did and it's what freaked me out the most. You've probably already guessed that my dad was a bad influence on my younger years. He got me mixed up in all sorts of stuff, but even when I was old enough to choose for myself, nothing changed." Why was he telling her this? "So when Peter said this guy, Jesus, who was also the creator of the universe, died to take the blame for all the stuff that I'd done, that messed me up."

"So you never got past that?"

"Oh no, I got past it. That's what I mean. I became a Christian and started devouring the Bible. Those Old Testament stories about the different guys who God used. They were a bunch of screwups too. But he still chose to use them, and those who decided to love him back got so much more." He hadn't expected to see tears shining in her eyes.

"What changed all of that?"

"I went on a mission with the wrong guy. Out there, you have to trust each other. We had gone out to gather information, but my partner saw an opportunity to take some of the bad guys out. I refused. There were too many risks to the surrounding community, but he did it anyway."

His voice cracked, and he turned his head away and stared into the fire. He hadn't told anyone this story before, but he couldn't stop himself.

"He killed a couple of kids. I sat with this one boy and watched the life drain out of his eyes and I could do nothing. When we got back to base and debriefed, he laid all the blame at my feet. Said that if I had helped him, the kids wouldn't have been killed. And I just … I failed."

"What do you mean?"

"Jesus took all the blame for everyone. And it didn't matter whether they accept it or not. He still took it. He died equally for everyone. And there I was, being given all the blame, and I was so angry I wanted to kill that guy. I wished he'd been on that bridge instead of those kids. I couldn't bring myself to forgive him or show mercy or grace. That's when I realized it was too late for me."

Neither one of them spoke for a long minute, then Emily said, "You know God's grace is free. You don't earn it. The reason Jesus took all that blame is because he's the only one who is able to. We can't do it. You can't do it."

"I know that. But I'm talking about after the fact. We're supposed to be made new, and all I could see was the bad stuff in me. Emily, I'm not a good person."

"So you really believe in this whole bad-boy persona you put on?"

"You say that like I have control over it."

"Don't you?"

"Maybe if I tried hard enough, but it's all I know. And now you want to fix me, don't you?"

Emily laughed. "Kinda, yeah. But only because I believe there is a person inside of you who is made for better things, and he's just been lied to for a lot of years."

He looked into her eyes and was pretty sure if he didn't do something quick, he'd kiss her. And he wanted it too badly to let it happen. "I should go."

"It's still early."

He smiled to cover his concern. "I know, but you've had a traumatic day, and it will be best if you have an early night."

Emily walked him out and couldn't help leaning toward him when he turned around at the door to say goodbye. "You want a lift back to the grocery store?"

"Nah, I'll walk back. It's not far."

"But it's freezing."

"I don't mind."

He found he was now closer to her than when he first walked out the door but wasn't sure how it had happened. The firelight flickered behind her, creating a halo around her figure. She moved a fraction closer and he lost himself. He leaned the rest of the way forward and kissed her. It should have only been a moment before he stopped it, but his mind couldn't get through the buzz that filled his body.

Emily was the first to pull away and only dipped her head to separate their lips.

His arms were around her and he couldn't remember putting them there. "I should get going," he whispered, still close enough to feel her breath.

"Okay. Stay warm," she whispered back.

It took all his willpower to step back and not follow her into the house. Thank goodness for the cold. He left his jacket open and jogged back to the parking lot, letting the brisk air dig deep into his bones.

He shouldn't have done that and now he'd pay for it.

Emily closed the door and leaned against it. She had underestimated him. She had underestimated herself.

After hearing his story, she felt closer to him than she'd felt to anyone in a long time. With Liam, she could open up and he would understand her pain. And that kiss. The world exploded around her when they touched, and that couldn't be undone.

She went back to the fire and sat down. *God, is this you? I can't afford to make a mistake here. I can't afford to open up my heart to the wrong person.*

But she knew that while she was surrounded by the euphoria that Liam left behind, it would be too hard to hear what God had to say, so she chose to enjoy the moment and worry about the consequences tomorrow.

Liam's face and hands were numb by the time he got home, and the cold didn't help as much as he had hoped. But he knew now that he couldn't follow through. And after Emily made it clear she'd call the cops if she ever knew someone was in trouble, he couldn't risk telling her. Even if he made her promise not to tell the police, he couldn't be sure she wouldn't. She was stubborn enough to do what she thought was necessary.

There had to be another way to satisfy Kyle, even if it meant offering him allegiance. But would that be enough for Kyle?

He gathered a few items of clothing that were scattered round and shoved them into his bag. The first thing he had to do was get out of town. He had to leave Emily behind before it was too late.

His phone vibrated in his pocket, and he closed his eyes, taking several deep breaths before looking at it. He both hoped and dreaded that it was Emily. But when he unlocked his phone, he saw it was a video message from Kyle. Liam's stomach tightened. He hadn't asked for more proof that Sophie was okay, and Kyle wasn't the generous type.

He tapped play and turned up the volume as he walked around the living room, watching when Sophie appeared on the screen with her arms tied together and a purple bruise easily visible on her cheek.

She looked up at someone behind the camera, nodded, then looked at the screen as a tear trailed down her face.

"Uncle Liam, I'm supposed to tell you that you're running out of time." She shifted and looked up over the camera again. Her face scrunched up as more tears fell, and this time her words were choked with them. "He said if you don't get him what he wants, he's going to take me apart." She sputtered, then whimpered. "Piece by piece."

The clip ended and Liam spun around and punched the wall.

Chapter 16

EMILY RUBBED the sleep from her eyes and stared up at the ceiling, still thinking about that kiss. It was a welcome change to the unease or sometimes terror that she woke up from.

She reached for her phone to check the time and saw that a message had come through from Liam. She couldn't ignore the leap in her chest and didn't want to. It was an invitation to dinner, and she had already typed back a positive reply but paused before hitting send. If she went to dinner, it could change everything. Up until that point, their contact could be reasoned away as platonic. Even the kiss could have been a whim. But this dinner wasn't that. This was a date. He would kiss her again and then she'd find herself involved with a man for the first time in years, and she had no way of knowing if she was prepared for that.

She lifted her phone to check the time again. Her dad wasn't her first choice for asking about relationship advice, but he would be overprotectively honest, and overprotective was about all she trusted right now. If she talked to Stacey about it, all Emily would get was a firm shove in Liam's direction, and she was already doing that to herself.

She brought a coffee down with her to the house and stopped outside the backyard to admire the large elm tree in the backyard. The new leaves coming out were vibrant and beautiful, and she wondered why she hadn't noticed them before. A soft smile played on her lips as her thoughts turned to Liam. After a moment, she shook it off and headed for the house, finding her dad sitting in his La-Z-Boy reading the newspaper.

"Well, hello there. What brings you by so early?"

"Can't I come have a coffee with my dad before he leaves for work?"

"Sure, have a seat." He folded his paper and tossed it on the small table beside him. "So let's have it."

"What?"

"Whatever is bothering you. Is it Liam?"

She took a sip of coffee to hide the smile that threatened at hearing his name.

His eyes widened and he said slowly, "Is that a yes?"

"Does Liam bother *you*?"

"That's a strange thing to ask. Isn't your opinion of the man what's most important?"

"I thought you'd be jumping at the chance to share your thoughts. Isn't that what dads want?"

"Okay, fine, that's very generous of you, but I'm not sure what it is you want me to say?"

"How about the truth?"

"I don't know him well enough to make an informed

decision, but I trust him enough *not* to dissuade you from seeing him again if he asks."

"He asked me to dinner."

"And?"

"And I don't know if I should go."

"Wait a second. You're asking your father if you should go on a date?"

"That's what I said. You should be ecstatic at the chance to interfere."

"Something's not right here."

Emily clacked her fingernails on the side of her cup. Her dad was maddeningly right. This was weird. "Okay, different question. Just tell me what you think about him. In general. Not in relation to your daughter."

"He saved your life, so my opinion is probably skewed by that."

"But you don't get any weird vibes?"

"Sweetheart, when I met your mom, I fell madly in love and ignored all the warning bells that something was wrong. I was probably in too dark of a place to even notice, and I thought she was the answer to all my problems. I was wrong. But she gave me you, so I have no regrets."

"I'm not sure where you're going with that."

"If you're going after Liam in order to fix something that's broken, don't."

"Right."

"But even if you make a mistake, good can still come out of it."

"So you think Liam is a mistake?"

"That's not what I said. It sounds to me like you don't want this to happen."

"I'm undecided."

"Then my other piece of advice is that you can't hide forever. Now, I've got to get ready for work, so I hope that helped."

"Knowing you're here for me helps."

"That's very sweet of you to say. Makes an old guy like me feel pretty good."

She got up and kissed him on the forehead before heading back to her apartment, where she sat on the edge of her bed with her finger poised over the keyboard on her phone.

What was it keeping her from saying yes to Liam? She wasn't looking for him to solve her problems. That was the last thing she wanted. But he did make her feel safe. And her desire to say no was mostly connected to fear more than anything else. He was a nice guy and had opened up the previous night. And going to dinner didn't mean anything had to happen. They weren't dating now just because they had dinner.

She scrunched up her face so the words were blurred as she typed out her reply: *C you then.*

Liam stared at the reply. He'd been in this game long enough to know he had her, and it made him sick. He flicked back to the video, paused on Sophie's bruised face. Emily didn't deserve to have her heart broken, but Sophie didn't deserve to have her life stolen. Maybe after it was all over, he could send Emily a letter and explain his actions. But that wasn't fair to her. He didn't deserve her forgiveness for what he was about to do, treating her like she was nothing more than a mark, simply a commodity until her usefulness was through. He'd stay out of her life for good and let her hate him for the rest of her life.

He pushed every thought from his mind and headed down to the beach to collect driftwood. He had one more shot at this, and he had to make sure it worked.

Emily added the last of the new maple products to the website. The restaurant was only open for a few months in the year while the syrup was in production. It brought a good return, but the extra products they could push all year made sure that her dad was secure into his retirement. If he ever took it.

Her phone rang, and she almost didn't answer when she saw it was Mrs. Carson. The woman could talk for an hour nonstop if you weren't careful, but Emily loved her, so she made sure she had a ready response to excuse herself politely if necessary.

"Hi, Mrs. Carson. How're you doin' today?"

"Hello, dear. I'm doing fine. H-How is everything with you?"

"Oh, you're calling about the incident at the store? I'm doing fine. Thanks for checking on me."

"That must have been terrifying. Thank goodness Liam was there to rescue you."

Emily clicked through the product listing to make sure she had all the details right. "Yeah, I was lucky to have him there."

"Did that make it extra special?"

She spotted a spelling error on one of the candles and corrected it before making one last pass, clicking from item to item. "Make what extra special?"

"Your gift."

She stopped clicking. "Gift?"

There was a long pause and then, "Oh dear. I think I may have spoiled it. I thought he gave it to you yesterday, but I suppose after everything that happened. Oh, I've ruined everything."

"No, oh, you mean … the gift? Yes, it was lovely."

Mrs. Carson breathed out a giant sigh. "I'm so glad. I would never have forgiven myself."

"No harm done."

"You know I had a hand in that."

"You did?"

"Yes, Liam came to me for some advice to find out what gift would be good to give you. I told him how you used to make things out of driftwood."

"Really?"

"Don't you remember?"

"Yeah, I remember."

"Do you still do that? I hope so. I bet he gave you some really beautiful pieces."

"Yes. The driftwood was beautiful. Thank you for giving him such a thoughtful idea."

"Oh, it's nothing. You've done so much for us. I wanted you to have something special."

"Thank you. Listen, I've got to run. My dad needs a hand down at the shop."

"I'll leave you to it then."

Emily laid her phone gently on the desk and leaned back. Liam was getting her a gift. And not just any gift. She pictured him scouring the beaches to find the right pieces. She'd be able to tell if he went looking for something special or if he grabbed the first ones he saw, not that it would matter if he didn't. But if he made an effort, that would speak volumes about what he thought of her. Her cheeks warmed and instead of trying to escape it, she let the warmth fill her up. It had been a long time since she'd felt like this. Maybe it was time.

Emily stood in front of the full-length mirror hanging on the back of her door and closed one eye, then the other. Choosing clothes had never been this difficult.

She pulled off the sweater Stacey had brought with her and decided to stick with what she knew. After putting on a buttercup-colored blouse, she pushed back her shoulders to alleviate her nerves and presented herself to her friend who lounged on the couch.

"I saw him in the grocery store yesterday. He is very attractive. He probably can't even count how many chin-ups he can do," she said before stuffing her mouth full of chips.

"He's okay."

Stacey blew a raspberry that had a hint of crumbs.

"You must really like him if you're lying to yourself like that."

"Even if I like him, he's still risky."

"So?"

"So I don't do risky. That was my problem in New York, remember? I was attracted to the wrong guy, and it blew up in my face."

She had never told anyone the full story. But telling people it was all down to a bad relationship was the easiest thing, and it was believable. Probably more believable than the truth.

"Besides, I can't really call it a date yet. It's dinner."

"It's definitely a date. He got you a gift. Now hurry up and get changed or else you'll be late."

"This is what I'm wearing." She held her arms out and spun.

"What? Why?"

"What's wrong with this?"

"It's not sexy at all."

"That's not the look I'm going for."

Stacey jumped off the couch and grabbed the collar of Emily's blouse. "I'm not saying you have to dress inappropriately, but you can at least look like you're not trying to be a nun." She unbuttoned the three buttons that enclosed Emily's throat, revealing the necklace chain. "There. That's much better."

Emily sucked in one of her cheeks and redid a button. "I'd rather not look desperate."

"No one could ever mistake you for desperate. Listen, I'm sorry I'm so pushy. I just hate to see you on your own."

"I'm fine on my own."

"I know, but wouldn't it be fun to be in love?"

"Didn't we already have this discussion? Being in love won't fix me. It won't make me a better person, and I sure hope it's not what I need to be happy. I don't want to *need* to have a guy in order to be happy."

Stacey took her friend's hand and pulled her down onto the couch. "I'm sorry if you think I'm trying to fix you. I care about you, and I do want you to be happy, but you're right. You can't rely on Liam for that."

"Thank you."

"So, how about you just go have fun with a nice guy? Not to solve your problems, but just to have a nice evening."

"That's what I'm trying to do."

"Okay then, I'm glad that's settled."

Emily checked the time. "I thought the afternoon would be slow, but it's time to go. Wish me luck."

"You won't need it. Just be yourself." She squeezed Emily's hand and then slapped her butt as she they went out the door.

Chapter 17

WHEN EMILY REACHED Liam's house, the sun had dipped behind the hill, bruising the sky. It was a beautiful time to be up here. She stopped to admire the purple strokes made by wispy clouds before walking up the steps to the porch.

She noticed the top step was a lighter color than the rest. She bounced on it. He must have replaced the nearly rotting step. Progress.

"Hi there," Liam said, coming outside to greet her.

"Hi." Her cheeks flushed.

"It's nice to have you visit under different circumstances." He held the door open for her and she paused at the door.

"Are all these candles for mood lighting, or haven't you bothered to connect the electricity?"

"Bit of both. I forgot to ring today until it got dark and then it was too late, but I found a barbecue in the shed that only needed a bit of cleaning, so I've got us covered. As long as you're not a vegetarian."

"I am," she said with a frown.

"Oh."

Liam looked so forlorn she couldn't continue the charade. "Kidding. I'm a big fan of red meat."

"That was just plain old mean. Man, small-town girls are brutal."

Emily shrugged and looked around the room. A folding table and two camp chairs were set up in the middle of what would have been the living room. With the candlelight flickering, it was cozy instead of sparse.

"Can't make it easy for the big-city boys rolling in and thinking we're easy pickings."

"Certainly not. Can I get you a glass of wine?"

"You don't have to offer me wine. That must be terrible for you."

"Why?"

"Because of AA."

"Oh, uh, yeah." He didn't usually make a slip like that. "No, it's fine, really. I just want you to be comfortable."

"Well, I'm comfortable sober."

"You sure?"

"Yes. Is there anything I can do to help you prepare dinner?"

"There's a prepackaged salad in the cooler over there if you want to grab a bowl from the kitchen and throw it in. I'll get the steaks started."

Emily headed for the cooler in the corner of the room and noticed a pile of driftwood on top of the bureau she had made. Was she not meant to see these yet? She wouldn't pretend she hadn't seen them, so she picked up a piece and looked it over. He'd chosen well.

"What do you think?" Liam said from the door.

"You mean the wood?"

"Yeah. I took a walk today and found those pieces. I don't know why, but there's something about them that speaks to me."

"Yeah. I, uh, I like driftwood too."

"Really? Huh. I don't think I've ever met anyone else who thinks of it as anything other than clutter on the beach."

Emily pushed her tongue into her cheek. "I used to make stuff with driftwood."

"Used to?"

"I haven't in a while."

"You should take some of that, then. I'd love to see what you do with it."

"Maybe." She decided not to push it. Instead she opened the lid of the cooler that contained a bottle of milk and a package of cheese and ham besides the salad. "So, there's a bowl in the kitchen?"

"Yeah. I'm not sure what, but all the kitchen stuff is still in there from my dad." He went back to the barbecue.

She looked at the wood again, confused. He had obviously used Mrs. Carson's information, not as a gift idea, but to endear himself to her. But he didn't need to do that. Couldn't he tell she already liked him? Why would he lie about it? It put her on edge.

A sizzle of meat hit the grill and Emily retreated into the kitchen. It was dark in there, so she pulled out her phone and used the flashlight to search through cupboards. She started on the left and worked her way across until she reached the cupboard above the stove and found a bottle of whiskey. It could have been Richard's. She pressed a hand to her forehead. She hoped it was Richard's, but when she pulled the bottle down and checked it, there was no dust.

She put it back where she found it and closed the cupboard. She gripped the edge of the sink, breathing deeply to settle her quickening heart. Fear multiplied her pulse, but the anger that followed buried her concern. He was a confident man who did not need to lie to her, and yet she'd found two within the space of a couple of minutes.

She could hear Liam whistle and had to decide whether she'd walk out or let him explain.

"You find a bowl?" he called out to her.

She'd let the charade, whatever it was, go on a bit longer before demanding an explanation. It couldn't be as bad as the thoughts she was having. After finding the bowl, she carried the salad back to the table and set it down before joining him on the porch.

"All set," she said as he flipped the meat. He smiled at her and she leaned on the doorframe, crossing her arms. "Hey, I was thinking about how you said you were one year sober."

"Yeah. It feels really good."

"Could I see your chip?"

"My what?" He clicked the tongs at her.

"Your one-year sobriety chip. Can I see it?"

"Oh." He took in a deep breath. "I, uh, I didn't

bring it with me. It's back at my place down south. I don't carry it around with me. You know … I'd hate to lose it."

"Yeah." She walked to the railing, pulling her jacket tightly around her body, both from the cold and her suspicion. The dark expanse of the lake below was ominous for the first time.

Liam joined her. "Words gotten around town about the events at the store yesterday. I had people stopping me in the street and shaking my hand."

"Small towns have the biggest mouths."

He laughed. "That's what I like about living in the city. They're easy to hide in."

"Does that mean you have a reason to hide?"

"Like I said, we all have our secrets."

"True."

"You ready to eat? I think the steaks are done."

She nodded and went inside to sit down while he got the meat and followed her in.

Liam deposited the main course on the plates and collected the lamp he had been using outside, setting it in the middle of the table. She looked sad, and he had the sudden urge to hold her, an urge he quickly clamped down. It couldn't be done. He needed the pendant, and he needed it now.

She cut through the meat slowly, unsure of what to say.

Liam took a bite and after he swallowed, said casually with a nod, "You okay?"

"Sure." She absentmindedly hooked a finger on the

necklace and slid her finger down the chain while she chewed.

"That pendant. You said it meant a lot to you?"

She looked at him, then pulled it out from under her shirt and looked at it. "It does. It's one of the few genuine gifts I've ever been given. Why?"

"Well, it's my dad's, right?"

She dropped it onto her chest. "If you recognized it, why didn't you say?"

"When you didn't tell me, I thought maybe you were keeping it out of spite because of the way I'd treated you." There was no delicate way to do this. He'd just have to lie through his teeth and keep pushing.

She nodded. "I was afraid you'd want to take it. And I wasn't lying when I said it meant a lot to me."

"I wasn't ready to talk about it, anyway. It brought up a lot of stuff. Even though he'd always promised it to me, I wasn't even sure I wanted it." He took another bite.

"He did give you the house."

"Yeah, but it's all just stuff. I had never even seen this house before coming here, but that pendant he'd had ever since I was a boy. I guess when we lost touch, he forgot I wanted it."

"So, you're saying you'd like it back?"

"No, certainly not if it means something to you. But would you mind if I had a look at it?"

She hesitated, but finally lifted it over her head and handed it to him. She watched him hold it close to his face, admiring all the fine details. It was strange to not have the weight hanging around her neck.

"I don't want to keep it, but would you mind if I hung on to it for a day or two? It's kind of like visiting my dad again, you know?"

She thought of the driftwood and the whiskey and the lack of electricity. And since when did Liam want to feel close to his dad? Something wasn't right. Nothing added up, and she was tired of playing this game. "Actually, no. I'd like it back, please."

"Really?"

"Yes." She held out her hand, and his pulled back a fraction, and that's when she knew. She should have known it at the police station. It was after he saw it hanging around her neck that his attitude toward her changed. At the time, she hadn't made the connection.

She ignored the searing pain of betrayal in her chest. He had been playing a game with her from the beginning and letting her guard down meant she'd pay a price. But right now, all she wanted was to make sure he didn't win.

"Listen," she said. "If it really means that much to you, I think you should keep it."

"Yeah?"

"Yeah."

"That would be amazing. You're amazing." He reached a hand across the table to take hers. She forced herself to allow it.

"Would you mind, though, if I kept the necklace? That was actually a gift from a friend."

"Yeah, sure." Liam felt like he could breathe again.

"It's got a funny clasp." She held out her hand. "I'll get it undone."

Liam had a quick look at the clasp. It didn't look difficult, but he didn't want to say no to her and he didn't have a fingernail to push down the latch anyway. He kept his fingers wrapped around the pendant but handed her the end of the necklace.

She pretended to fiddle with it, leaning over the table and squinting in the low light. "Just a sec." She pulled it closer, and he moved with it, but loosened his grip enough that she was able to slip it out of his hand. He moved to grab it again, but she put it over her head and tucked it under the shirt before he understood what had happened. She stood and backed away from the table.

"It's valuable, right?" she said, keeping her back to the door as she moved closer. "That's why you're here? Richard told me it wasn't worth anything, but I knew he was lying. I could tell it was more valuable than he let on. But it didn't matter to me, because the value for me was in the sentiment."

"Emily." Liam stood. "I already told you you could keep it. You're the one who offered."

A part of her wanted to be convinced by him, but she wouldn't allow herself to be manipulated anymore. "Is that why he gave it to me instead of you? Because he wanted someone to have it who appreciated it instead of selling it for the money? I thought you cared about things that mattered. I will admit, you had me fooled. You are very good. Or maybe I wanted to believe your lies."

"I never lied to you."

"Camp chairs, folding tables, and candles? I thought you were planning on sticking around."

"I told you I haven't gotten around to it." She wasn't experienced in this. All he had to do was make her second guess and they'd be back on track. He could still do this. He had to.

"What about the whiskey in the kitchen?"

He closed his eyes. He'd forgotten that was in there. "I fell off the wagon. I didn't want to disappoint you."

He had an answer for everything. It was infuriating. "I spoke to Mrs. Carson today. I can't believe — " An incredulous laugh fell from her mouth. "It's embarrassing, but I was flattered that you sought her out to find out what special gift you could get me. But it was never about a gift, was it? You just wanted a way to make me trust you more so you could con me out of the pendant. I bet you couldn't believe your luck when I got into trouble at the store, and you got to be the one to save me. Or did you plan that too?"

"Emily, I didn't — "

"I can't believe I trusted you for one second. But you're nothing more than a criminal. Are you even Richard's son? Or did you fake that like you faked everything else?"

Liam dropped his head. He'd failed Sophie *and* Emily. Everyone lost. "It wasn't all fake."

"No? What part wasn't fake?" She pressed her lips together to stop them from trembling.

"I am Richard's son."

"Well, that's great. You want to know what wasn't

fake for me? That kiss. Boy, that felt real. To me anyway."

"Emily — "

"No, you don't get to have a say. I can't trust anything that comes out of your mouth. But I guess I should thank you. You reminded me that the world is indeed a horrible place that I need to protect myself from." She threw her arms out to the side. "No damage was done besides my hurt pride, so I guess I got out of it a bit better this time."

"I'm sorry."

"I. Don't. Believe you."

He nodded. "Okay, that's your right. But please. I need that pendant."

"Are you serious right now? Why? You owe someone money?"

"Yes. Dangerous men."

Fear for his safety nudged her hand toward the necklace, but he didn't deserve her care or concern. "Good. Serves you right. Next time, make better choices." She stormed out of the house with Liam chasing after her.

"Emily, please. You don't understand. This is really important." He grabbed her arm. She ripped it away.

"Don't you dare touch me. You could have come clean with me at the start. Before you hurt me. Before I hated you."

"You hated me from the start."

"No, I was angry at you. There's a difference. If you had asked for the pendant when we first met, you would have had a better chance of getting what you wanted. But you made me care for you. You got through my walls and took advantage of me. You lied and manipulated me and I can't — " She choked on the last word. "Now you get nothing." She swung around and ran for her truck, blinded by tears she didn't want him to see.

Liam slammed his hand against the side of the house. He could have run after her, held her down, and taken the necklace. She would have called the police and they would have chased after him, but he could have had a chance. But he couldn't bring himself to do it. Not that. He'd done too much to hurt her, and now he had nothing.

He tipped his head back and looked up at the stars and wondered if God was really up there. He knew there was darkness inside of him, but to see what he was capable of, the way he'd been willing to treat Emily even when he cared for her … Jesus may have given up his life for the likes of someone like him, but Liam had proven time and again that he was too far gone. He had no soul left to save.

Chapter 18

EMILY WOULD HAVE GONE HOME and slammed every door in the house, but her dad would see her come home early and hear the fallout, and when he came to check on her, he'd end up brokenhearted. So she drove herself to Stacey's instead. Her cynical wit would be the healing balm she needed.

Tony opened the door with his shirt on inside out and backward. "Emily? I thought you had a date?"

"I did. Am I interrupting something? 'Cause I can go."

"Uh … " She could see he wanted to say yes but didn't know if he was allowed.

"Emily?" Stacey appeared down the hall, buttoning up her shirt. "What's going on? Is everything okay? Tony, why haven't you invited her in?"

Emily took a step back. "I'm sorry. I shouldn't have interrupted your night. I'll come back later."

"No, you won't. Come in." Stacey whispered in Tony's ear. Whatever she said pleased him enough that he disappeared with a smile on his face. She ushered Emily into the living room.

"I'm so sorry. I shouldn't have come here."

"Is something wrong?"

"Yes, but — "

"Then don't worry about it. Tony's fine."

"I don't know what you could have said to him, and I don't want to know."

"All you need to know is I look after my man. He has no complaints. Now, tell me what happened."

After hearing of Emily's night, Stacey sat quietly for a moment before saying, "You want me to shoot him? Because I will. I wouldn't do it for anyone else, but I'd do it for you."

"No, I don't need you to shoot him. But thanks for saying you would."

"I was worried he was too good-looking to be true."

"No, you weren't."

"Okay, you're right. I had hoped he would help you get out of your funk."

"I'm not in a funk. I'm just having trouble figuring out life."

"No, you're definitely in a funk. You're like … I don't know. Like an icy fire instead of a hot one."

"I'm totally messed up."

"No, not totally, just a little. But we all are a little, right?"

"But you think I'm more messed up than others. Heck, I *know* I'm more messed up than others."

"Like I said before, I just want you to be happy, and I thought Liam might do that, but I got it so completely wrong that I threw you into the arms of someone who did the exact opposite."

"I threw myself. I'm a grown woman and it was my choice."

"I'm so sorry that happened to you, but on a completely different subject, how much do you think that pendant is worth?"

Emily laughed. "Always helping me keep my focus on what matters most."

"Hey, I just want to keep things in perspective."

Emily lifted the pendant off her chest and looked at it from all angles. "I have no idea. But it must be a lot."

"Must be more than a house if he hasn't sold — Wait. That's it. I've got it. I'm about to make you the happiest woman alive." She let out one bursting laugh, then slammed her hand across her mouth.

"What?"

"This is so perfect. We thought this thing with Liam was bad, but it's so, so good."

"What are you talking about? You've gone mental."

"Hear me out. You said Liam is desperate for that pendant because he owes someone money."

"Yes."

"So give it to him."

"You want me to give it to him after the way he treated me? After you said you'd commit murder? You are not the Stacey I know and love."

"No, you won't give it to him out of the kindness of your heart. You're going to give it to him as an exchange."

"For what? He has nothing I want. In fact, I'm pretty sure he has nothing."

"He has a house."

Emily's mouth dropped open. "You're right. Why didn't I see that before? He did say he was really Richard's son. So he really does own the house. And this pendant has to be worth more than that house if he didn't just sell it himself to pay these guys back."

"You are slow to the party, but I'm glad you arrived."

Emily jumped forward and gave her friend a hug. "You are brilliant. I can't believe this. I'm going over there right now, and I'm going to get myself my dream home. And tell Tony thanks for letting me interrupt your evening."

"Oh, I will. Don't you worry."

Liam jumped out of his chair when he heard the car pull into his driveway. He knew it wasn't Emily and was both disappointed and relieved. But if it wasn't Emily, then the question remained of who would be paying him a visit.

He pushed back the screen door and looked out. A metallic blue Mustang was parked right next to the porch. Liam's face tightened. As did every muscle in his body. He didn't need to see the driver to know who it was that would drive a car like that to his doorstep.

"Not a bad little spot you've got here," Kyle said when he exited the car. He inhaled the fresh air. "Not often you get to breathe something so pure."

"Why are you here?"

"I take it that's a rhetorical question?"

"I told you I was handling it."

Kyle jogged up the steps. "Shall we discuss things inside? It's a bit nippy out here. I'm too acclimatized to the North Carolina weather these days."

Liam turned and went inside without holding the door open.

"I like what you've done with the place. It's very minimalist. And the candles add a nice touch. Very romantic. You must have been expecting me." He ran a finger across the fireplace mantle, rubbing his fingers together and flicking away the dust they'd accumulated.

"Tell me why you're here so you can leave."

"I think I've been very generous. I've afforded you more time than I would most, but I can't help but feel you've taken advantage of my kindness to you."

"Kindness?"

"I give your niece food and a place to stay, and you've caused her to overstay her welcome."

"If you've hurt — "

"I want my pendant, Liam. That's all. I thought you were capable of such a simple assignment. You used to be a dependable guy. But I guess things have changed."

"I'm working on it. But if there's something else I can give you instead, I might be able to work a bit faster.

I've got more vases. I might be able to get my hands on a nice painting or two."

"Are you saying you can't hold up your end of the deal?"

"No. I'm just saying, if you're in a hurry, there may be other options available."

"I want the pendant. Is it still with the same person it was last time we talked?"

"Kyle."

"Tell me who has it, and I'll get it myself."

Emily had worked herself up so much that she had to pull over on the side of the road and wait for the giddiness to settle. She was relieved she wouldn't have to be angry with him this time. They could have a cordial conversation where everyone got what they wanted.

But when she pulled into his driveway and saw the Mustang, a flash of anger seared through her. The whole time he'd been here, he'd ridden around on that bike and now, suddenly, he brings a fancy Mustang out of hiding. She had had enough of Liam's secrets and would be relieved when this was all over.

She shook her arms out when she got out of the car and let the fire in her belly give her the confidence to pull off the best move of her life. So why didn't it feel like all her dreams were coming true? She kept her hand on the door handle.

Okay, God, I was quick with this move and didn't check with you. If you don't want me to go through with this, can you let me know? Her mind was too jumbled up to hear anything clearly that might resemble direction from God. *Scratch that. I'm going to follow through on this, but if I'm getting this wrong, please protect me from my mistakes.*

She felt the sudden urge to run away, but that was fear, not prompting, and now she was more confused than ever.

But she wanted that house, so she stowed the pendant in the glove box, just in case, and headed for the house that would soon be hers.

"Come on, Liam. Why the hesitation? I'm offering to take the entire problem off your hands. You'll still get Sophie back."

Both men turned to the door when they heard footsteps.

"Liam? You home?"

Kyle pulled his gun and stepped backward, holding it behind his back. "Didn't know you were expecting company."

"Liam?" Emily knocked on the door.

"Ignore her, she'll go away," Liam whispered to Kyle. He felt like he'd eaten a pile of rocks.

"Liam," Emily continued. "I have a proposition for you I think you will be very interested to hear."

Kyle's eyebrows lifted. "Oh, I'm interrupting something. No wonder you haven't gotten the pendant back yet. You've been distracted. Don't you want to find out what her proposition is?"

"No," Liam hissed through his clenched teeth.

Kyle shrugged. "I sure am curious," he said louder than was necessary. He moved from the shadows into the flickering light. "Come in," he called out.

Emily walked through the door and stopped when she saw the two men. Then Liam watched as her eyes locked on Kyle, and her face changed from an angry glow to deathly white. Her shoulders curved forward, and she wrapped her arms around herself. It was hard to tell in the shaking light, but it looked like she was trembling.

Kyle put a fist on his hip. "Emily Peterson? It can't be. Is the light playing tricks on me?"

Emily choked on a sob that tried to escape her throat and Liam took a couple of quick steps over to her. "What's going on?" he whispered close to her ear.

"She's fine. Just surprised to see me. It's been such a long time. But we're good friends, aren't we, Emily?"

She shook her head and cowered toward Liam.

"Ouch. That's too bad. You've really looked after yourself. Not the fresh-faced little girl I met in New York. More experienced these days, hey? I like that in a woman." He took a step forward and she shrank back.

"Don't you dare touch me."

Liam moved in front of her, and she grabbed hold of his sleeve and pulled herself closer.

Liam squared his shoulders. "Kyle, I think you better go."

A smile slid up Kyle's face. "Oh, no way. We used to share a lot back in the day, but I don't think we've ever shared a woman before." He wagged his finger toward them. "So I was right. You got sidetracked. You're getting a little on the side and didn't want to cut your trip short? Can't say I blame you."

"Kyle, if you want what you came for, then you better leave. Now."

"Fine. But I'm coming back tomorrow for what you owe me." He lifted his gun and pointed it at Liam's head. "I'll get what I want one way or the other."

He walked toward the door with the gun still aimed, and Liam reached behind to move Emily around and keep himself between her and the gun.

"Nice to see you again, Emily." Kyle winked before he walked out the door. "You two have a nice evening."

When Kyle's car door closed, Emily exhaled all her breath and collapsed onto the floor. Liam dropped down beside her. At first he had to remind her to breathe, but then she sucked air into her lungs in quick, choking gasps.

"Hey, okay, slow it down or you'll pass out."

She was lost inside her nightmare and couldn't hear him. She tried to get up and escape, but he held onto her. She began throwing out her arms. "No! Let me go! I have to get out of here." She couldn't see or understand. All she could think of to do was run.

Liam gripped her tightly. "Emily, you're safe. He's gone. You're safe. Shh."

Her eyes locked on to his for a moment and the fog

cleared enough that she remembered where she was, and she stopped thrashing.

He rocked her while she whimpered into his shoulder. "You're safe now. He won't hurt you. I won't let him."

"There was — there was so much blood."

"Blood? Where? When? Did he do something to you?"

"I did it — " She choked on her sobs.

"Hey, shh." He pulled her tighter. "I've got you. I won't let anything happen to you. Not again. I won't let anyone hurt you again."

Chapter 19

EMILY GULPED down the water Liam handed her after she was settled on the dusty couch. "Better?" He brushed his finger along her forehead and tucked her hair behind her ear.

"Yeah. Thank you."

"So you know Kyle." He didn't hide the pain in his voice.

She closed her eyes and rested the glass in her lap. "Before I tell you anything, I need you to be honest with me. I need to ask you something, and I need the truth."

"I promise. Whatever it is."

"Did Kyle send you here for me?"

"No. No way. I didn't even know you two knew each other until tonight. I swear. He came for me, not you."

"I can't believe this is happening. I keep expecting to wake up and find it's all a dream. But it's not." She looked up at him. "Is it?"

"I wish it was." He reached over to put a hand on

her knee but changed his mind. "Was he the reason you left New York?"

"Yes."

Liam shook his head. "He was the bad boy you fell for. I'm surprised you would have gone for a guy like that."

"I didn't. I mean, that's what I tell people, that I fell for the wrong guy. I was attracted to him and it's what part of me wanted, but we didn't date or anything."

"Oh, so you just … "

Her head rocketed around toward him with fire in her eyes. "No. That's not what happened. He — " Her throat closed off her words and she pressed her face into her hands.

"Oh."

"I was stupid and naïve, and I didn't know what I was doing. No, that's not the truth. I'm so tired of hiding from the truth." She stood up, trying to escape the weight she'd been carrying for so many years. The thing she had spent the last years thinking she was safe from.

When she turned around to face him, he was leaning forward with his elbows on his knees. The sincere concern and regret showing on his face gave her courage. "You don't have to hide anymore, Emily."

She sat back down. "I thought I was immune from it in a way. I'd grown up never meeting anyone like Kyle, and I couldn't imagine the kind of things that went on outside of my little town. But I was so angry and numb I wanted to feel anything else instead of what I had to put up with growing up. I didn't know how bad things could really get."

"Being assaulted like that is a terrible evil. I'm sorry you had to go through that."

She shook her head. "It wasn't only that." She didn't know if she could trust him, but who better to offer a full confession to than someone who's probably seen worse. "I was angry at my mom. I wanted to get back at her. She was the main reason I wanted to escape Oakridge in the first place, so when I got an opportunity to work with a furniture maker in the city, I took it. I told myself that God had opened up an incredible opportunity for my life. It may have been true, but that's not the real reason I went. It was to pay her back. And the whole time I was away, she guilt-tripped me into returning. She didn't like that she couldn't control me."

"She did something?"

"You could say that. We had this massive fight over the phone one day, and I ended up hanging up on her. An hour later, my dad rang back and told me she was in the hospital after a stroke. I thought she was faking it."

"She would do that?"

"She's pretended to be ill to get her own way before, yes."

"I'm so sorry."

"I had made some friends while I was there who were different from anyone back home. These guys were fun, and I wanted to have fun. I was tired of being the good girl all the time. Doing what she told me to do.

"We'd go party a lot and at one of these parties, I was introduced to Kyle. He laid it on thick, but he was smooth. Told me how beautiful I was and even though I knew deep down that he was bad news, I'd never felt special before like that. I'd never had someone so good-looking and confident tell me I was special. He knew just what to say."

"Sounds like him." Liam couldn't ignore the cruel irony that he'd treated her the same.

"But there was always that thing deep inside that warned me away from him, so I never took him up on any of his invitations. Not until that phone call. I lost it. I wanted to prove to her that she couldn't manipulate me anymore. I thought a good way to do that would be to turn up to this party Kyle had told me about." She scoffed. "I could have gone and gotten a tattoo or something instead. My mom always said they were of the devil. But I was feeling pretty low about myself, and I thought hearing all the nice things Kyle would say to me would make me feel better. I thought, what harm would it do?" She started crying again and Liam put a hand on her back.

"I'm sorry he did that to you." Liam was glad she couldn't see his face at that moment. It would have been murderous. If Kyle didn't have Sophie, he would have returned Emily to her dad and gone and done something he would have only partially regretted.

"I was always careful before that." She sniffed. "I always went with my friends who looked out for me. We looked out for one another. I would never have done it if I wasn't so mad at my mom. I was so stupid."

"And the blood?"

She twitched. "What blood?"

"You said there was so much blood."

"When?"

"When you were on the floor." Her shoulders curved in again. "Hey, listen. If you don't want to say, that's fine. But this thing, whatever it is, is eating you alive. Now, I've seen a lot of bad stuff and I've done plenty myself. If you want to tell me, whatever it is, I can take it and I won't judge you."

"I've tried." She sobbed. "I've tried so hard to handle it. I go to church every Sunday and I raise my hands and I beg God to take it away, but it still feels like it happened yesterday. It won't leave me alone."

A swelling darkness grew in the pit of Liam's stomach. He had thought her trauma was based on Kyle's assault, but he feared the story didn't end there.

As he watched her trying to get ahold of herself again, he wanted desperately to take away her pain. He took hold of her hand instead and out of nowhere came a memory of something Peter had said to him. It was a scripture, and he couldn't imagine how he'd remembered it. He tried to shake it, but it wouldn't go. He gave in to his urge to speak it.

"Listen, this might be stupid, but there's this verse in the Bible that says if we confess our sins to each other, we can be healed. At least I think it's in the Bible."

A small laugh escaped through the tears. "Yes, that's in there. I can't believe you of all people are reciting the Bible to me."

"What can I say? I'm a man of many talents and those words meant a lot to me once."

"But not anymore?"

"I don't know. If we're being honest with each other, I'm still thinking about it. But listen. You can tell me.

I'm not going to tell anyone. God knows all the things I've done. And I'm not from a small town, so I don't have a big mouth."

She laughed again, then sniffed. "Maybe you're right."

"Hang on." He ran to the bathroom and came back with a wad of toilet paper. "To clean up."

"This is the weirdest friendship I've ever had." She wiped her face.

"You don't know how glad I am to hear you say that."

"What, that you're weird?"

"No, the friend part. I thought you hated me."

"That's why it's weird. You may be the only person I know that I feel like I can talk to about this." But she still felt the horror of telling him her darkest secret. One that she couldn't even fully understand herself. "Will you do something for me first?"

"If I can, yeah."

"Tell me something you did. I need to know you have that same place as I do, where all of your nightmares come from."

Liam let out a slow, sad breath and leaned back on the couch. He'd never been so confronted in his life. "You don't know what you're asking."

"I'm pretty sure I do."

It would expose parts of himself that he'd never dreamed he would lie bare for anyone. He had to consider for a moment if it was too much of her to ask. He couldn't even look at her as he tried to put the words together in his mind. If he spoke them, that would make it real, and it was the thing he feared the most. Like Emily said, it was the place where all his worst nightmares came from. He finally got the courage to look her in the eye and what he saw was such a genuine earnestness, a deep compassion that already looked deep into his soul. He held his breath. If the circumstances had been any different, he would have kissed her and never stopped.

"Okay." He focused all his energy on speaking the words he never thought he'd be brave enough to say. "Kyle may be a terrible person, but I'm the one who made him that way."

Chapter 20

EMILY HAD to remind herself to blink. She didn't know whether to slap him or tell him he was ridiculous. "I don't quite understand how you could be responsible for Kyle's behavior."

"I've known him for a long time. When I was a kid and my dad would use me in his cons, he'd always make sure I took the fall because I was a kid and wouldn't stay in jail long. I hated him for it. I hated having to pay for his crimes and I hated that he enjoyed it."

"I didn't know that. I knew your dad had regrets, but he never told me what they were."

"No, he wouldn't have told you. But it was in juvie where I met Kyle and we started hanging out together. He gave me the opportunity to get out from underneath my dad. We made our own money. We started out stealing small stuff and doing cons here and there. Then there was this guy." Liam squeezed his hands together and tried to swallow but his mouth was dry. "We knew him from around the place. He was a very scary guy.

We'd heard stories but didn't know which ones were true. Kyle wanted to steal something from him. It was a watch, I think. I wanted nothing to do with it, but he eventually convinced me. Then we got caught."

Emily could see that it cost Liam a lot to share this. "But you'd been to juvie before."

"It wasn't the police who caught us. This guy, I don't even remember his name, he caught us in his place. I had never been so terrified in my entire life, and I didn't even know why at the time. But the guy had a deep darkness in his eyes. They were like black holes that contained no humanity.

"Anyway, he set up his own little trial. I thought for a moment that we got lucky. I mean, I'd talked my way out of a lot of trouble. I could talk my way out of this. But then he told us things. Told us what he wanted to do to us and gave us the chance to accuse each other. Kyle kept his mouth shut." Liam shook his head. "I don't know how or why. Maybe if I hadn't spoken up, he would have, but I didn't give him the chance. I was so scared. And I told myself that it was Kyle's fault and I didn't want to be there in the first place. That's what I told myself before I gave Kyle up.

"The guy shook my hand and walked me out. Kyle didn't say a word as I left, and I didn't see him for days. I had nightmares every night. And then out of nowhere he was back, but he was a different person. He'd always been cocky, but now he was — I don't even know what to call it. Everything changed then. The stuff he got into after that had no limits."

"Did he do anything to you?"

"No. When he saw me, he acted like it was no big deal, said we were still friends, apologized for making me go. But I couldn't stomach the stuff he got into and we parted ways. So, as much as I know Kyle is a very bad guy, I can't help but feel responsible."

"That's why you triggered when that guy blamed you when you were in special forces?"

"Yeah."

"And after what your dad did … "

"Yeah, but if I hadn't done that to Kyle, he wouldn't have hurt you."

"You can't know that. You're not responsible for Kyle's choices, just like he's not responsible for yours."

"That's a nice thing to say, but nice doesn't cut it. There's nothing you can say that makes it okay. I don't mean that to sound harsh. It's just reality."

"I don't blame you."

"You don't have to. I carry enough blame for the two of us."

She picked at her fingernails. "You asked about the blood."

"You don't have to tell me."

"I think I killed someone. Maybe more than one."

"You think?"

"I was drugged at the time. Kyle drugged me. I found out later it was LSD. That's what happened at the party. Then he brought me somewhere … I don't even know … I only have snippets of memory of what happened next. I'm sure I don't have to explain."

"No."

"But then I was alone in the room, and I remember

leaning on a chair, trying to orient myself to get to the door. But before I could get there, the door opened and a bunch of people came in. I thought it was a party, and I was safe because I wasn't alone anymore. I fell into this one guy trying to explain what had happened, but I couldn't put the words together and the next thing I know, everyone was pulling at me, moving me, spinning me around until I was dizzy. I had this floating sensation of being moved about the room."

Liam's hand fisted in his lap. He knew exactly what had happened to her.

"Then I was sick and I think I threw up. I remember everyone moving back, but then I had a gun in my hand. I didn't even know what it was at first. I held it away from me and there was a bang and someone yelled. I was scared and I wanted to run, but with the chaos in the room I couldn't even figure out where the door was, and I still had this gun in my hand, and I heard more shots and — " She sucked in a sharp breath. "I remember — I remember the blood hitting me. It was hot and sticky." She took a breath. "I didn't remember that before." Her fingernails dug into her palm. "I couldn't see anyone anymore and I stumbled out into the daylight somehow. I don't remember finding the door or anything. The sunlight was just suddenly there, and all I could think to do was run."

"No wonder you came back home. Why didn't you go to the police?"

"I did."

"They didn't help you?"

"The police found me as I stumbled along in a daze.

A cop car pulled up beside me. I think I still had the gun in my hand because they got me on the ground and handcuffed me before taking me away."

Liam chewed on his lip. "Where you able to tell them everything you told me?"

"Mostly, I think."

"And?"

"They confirmed the blood that covered me wasn't mine. And they said there were at least two different DNAs. They did a rape kit and found Kyle's DNA, too, and brought him in."

"But Kyle didn't go to prison."

Emily shook her head. "It was my fault."

"I can't even fathom how you could think something like that."

"I found out my mom had passed away."

Liam closed his eyes, ashamed at how he'd treated her after all she'd been through.

"Kyle admitted to being with me, but said it was mutual. He said there were drugs at the party and thought I might have taken something but couldn't confirm or deny. He said he himself had not taken any drugs but had a lot to drink."

"And they believed him?"

"No, they wanted me to press charges."

"But your mom."

"I was numb but with this deep ache that I couldn't understand. Then Kyle sent someone to deliver a message to me. He said he knew about the blood and knew what I did, and if I didn't drop the charges against him, he would make sure the police knew too."

Liam couldn't stop fidgeting. "The police would have believed you over him. Where was your dad? Does he know all of this?"

Emily shook her head. "I didn't tell anyone. All I wanted was for the ground to swallow me up. And after hearing about my mom and Kyle's threats, I wanted it all to disappear. I wanted to forget forever. All of it. The assault, the gun, the blood. All of it. I wanted it to disappear. So I dropped the charges."

"What did the police say?"

"They weren't happy about it, but they couldn't find any bodies to match the blood and, without my allegations against Kyle, they had nothing. So I came home and I've been hiding here ever since. But it doesn't go away." Her tears were choking her throat again. "None of it has, and I have to live with the fact that I probably killed people."

"Those people deserved to die. They were there to buy you."

"What?"

"That's what he was doing with you. That image that you remember of being passed around. They were buyers examining you. I don't know how you got your hands on a gun, but it's what saved your life."

She sank back into the couch. "It had crossed my mind. I don't remember the police suggesting it, but they asked me a lot of questions to figure out where I was with Kyle. They wanted to know of any other associates of Kyle's I knew, which were none."

"Emily, I am so sorry for what I did to you. After

everything you've been through, and I've made things worse."

"Is it Kyle who wants the pendant?"

"Yeah."

"Why? What do you owe him money for? I thought you said you guys parted ways."

He saw a shift in her body away from him. She still didn't trust him, and he didn't blame her one bit. "Something I did cost him money."

"What?"

"Don't worry about it. It doesn't matter."

"So after all of this, after everything I've told you, you're going to keep it from me?"

"I don't want you to get hurt."

"It's too late for that. You owe me the truth."

He stood and walked across the room until he was in shadow. "I can't."

"Have you really done something that bad? Worse than what you've already told me?"

"No, it's just — I can't do this."

"What?"

"Be a good person." He took a few steps back toward her. "It doesn't matter what little good I do. I've been a liar my whole life. Ever since I was a boy. Sure my dad used me, but I liked it too. I was good, and I learned quickly that when you're honest with people, you get hurt."

"You get hurt," she said flatly.

"Yeah."

"And when you're a liar, you hurt others."

"Yeah, well, I never hung around long enough to see

that part. That was one of the first lessons my old man taught me — the importance of blowing off the mark. Don't get emotionally attached."

"I see."

He closed his eyes. "I never meant to hurt you."

"Never?"

He couldn't look at her. "At the start, I just needed the pendant, no matter what it cost. I knew someone would get hurt."

"And you've got to look after yourself."

"That's what I mean. It's who I am. Maybe that's why I ran away from Peter in the end."

"I don't mean to get all Christiany on you, but did it ever occur to you that perhaps God gave you those skills for another purpose besides a con? I mean, under different circumstances, you'd be able to do good."

"That's what Peter said. He knew how to make use of them too. I could gather a lot of intel for him and I'm exceptional at reading a room. I guess 'cause I've conned people for so long, I can usually tell when someone is lying and I often know why."

"But you chose the bad instead of the good."

"I don't know how to be that other person. I've tried. I'm sorry. If things were different. If I was different … " He ran his hand through his hair and kept his head bowed.

With all the trauma and emotion mixed up in the moment, Emily should have been a wreck, but her mind cleared as she watched Liam hiding half in the shadow. The world was made up of broken, messed-up people, and if you were lucky, you knew a God who could see the person he created you to be and who was willing to walk beside you and give you the strength to make better choices.

She stood. "I'll be right back."

He didn't move, just watched her go and waited, wondering if she'd really return.

When she did, she tossed him what she had been carrying.

He snatched the pendant from the air and looked down at it in his open palm. "Why are you giving me this?"

"I wish you would tell me what's going on, but even if you don't, no matter what you've done, I don't want you owing Kyle anything."

He closed his fingers around the pendant and held his breath. Heat radiated out of his center, but he fought it. He held out his hand. "I don't deserve this."

She looked at the pendant. "That's not why I gave it to you. None of us deserves a second chance and yet sometimes we get one. This may be your last opportunity to make things right. It's time to put everything as it should be, so you at least have the chance."

"Why?"

"Because that's what God did for me."

Liam had never been so lost in his life. Peter had offered him the same choice once, and he turned his back on it. He'd spent all these years hiding from the truth because he thought the truth was, he was worthless.

He tasted salt on his lips and reached a hand to his

face, wiping away tears. "What if I can't do it? What if I try and I screw it up?"

She walked up to him and took his hand. "We're all a bunch of screwups, remember? But God knows that already, and the only thing he's really interested in is where your heart is at right now."

He pulled his hand out of hers and swapped the pendant in his pocket for his phone. After unlocking it, he held it up for her to see. "That's my sister, Claire and her daughter, Sophie."

"Your niece. She's pretty."

"Kyle has her, and he wants the pendant in exchange for her life."

Emily's stomach lurched, but she didn't respond immediately. She squeezed her eyes tightly. "Why didn't you tell me?" she whispered.

"Because I couldn't risk you involving the police. He'd kill her. Or worse."

"You should have told me. You could have said not to call the police."

"And you wouldn't have?"

She wasn't sure of the answer. "So he just took her?"

Liam put his hand in his pocket and ran his finger over the smooth surface of the pendant. "I intercepted a truck full of women he would be auctioning off. It lost him a lot of money. He wants his money back. You can't call the police, Emily."

"Then go. Go now and save Sophie. And promise me. Promise me you'll think about what I said."

He touched the side of Emily's face, running his thumb

along her cheek. "I — " He wanted to say so many things but couldn't. Among them was "I'm sorry," but more than that, he wanted her to know how he felt about her. How much she meant to him, but how heartbroken he was knowing that he could never have her, not after everything that had happened. There was too much. She knew too much about the mess that was inside of him. "I don't know how I can ever say sorry enough for what I did to you."

"Don't say anything. Just go. Save Sophie."

Chapter 21

IT WAS cold on his motorcycle as he rode to the closest airport that would connect him to Charlotte, but after Emily had wrapped her arms around him to say goodbye, he still felt the warmth of her touch. If things had been different — he shook off the thought. All that did was distract him from his primary concern now, which was not just to get Sophie back, but also to get Kyle as far away from Emily as he could.

This time, he was lucky enough to get a quick flight with a short layover at JFK. He'd have to come back for his bike another time. Maybe he wanted a reason to return. That was another thought he had to clamp down on. Hope was a scary thing for a guy like him. Believing in a future that involved wholeness and love was beyond him at the moment. Right now, he couldn't allow himself to think beyond getting Sophie home. What came after that, he was afraid to imagine.

After collecting his ticket and clearing security, Liam marched down the concourse with his phone pressed against his ear. "I've got the pendant."

"That was quick. If I had known a visit would get you motivated, I would have come sooner." Kyle's voice lowered as though they were sharing a secret. "Is it Emily? Did she persuade you? I couldn't blame you. She's delicious."

"Emily's got nothing to do with it," he said through his teeth. "All I want is Sophie."

"You seem a bit touchy. Did you and Emily have a fight?"

"Can we stay on the subject, please?"

"All right. If you insist. Come into the city and —"

"I'll see you in Charlotte."

"But we're both in New York."

"Sophie's in Charlotte."

"After all we've been through together, and you don't trust me?"

"We meet in Charlotte. You bring Sophie for the exchange, or you don't get the pendant."

"You drive a hard bargain. Okay, I'll see you in Charlotte."

After hanging up the phone, Liam looked at the picture of Claire and Sophie. He'd wait to call his sister. He didn't want to get her hopes up until he had something concrete to give her.

When he reached the waiting area at the gate, he remained standing and looked at his watch. With an hour left until boarding, it would be impossible for him to stay in one place the way he was wound tight. He wouldn't relax again until Sophie was safely at home.

He hefted his bag onto his shoulder and kept walking until he reached the windowed end of the terminal. He stood and watched a plane take off, his thoughts shifting from Sophie and Claire to Emily. Claire would like Emily. There was an irony in Emily's sense of humor that reminded him of his sister. Brian would like her too. You could tell from her smile that she was a genuine person. He remembered the first time she smiled at him. The way her freckles brought an innocence to the expression. He'd never met anyone like her before. He'd never *felt* like this about anyone before. Why had life brought her to him now, in the middle of this, just to snatch her away again? Or was it God? Was God punishing him by showing him what he could have had? He'd never know. But one thing was certain: He would miss her, and he could do nothing to change that.

"I love watching the planes coming and going."

Liam was startled and turned to the speaker.

"Sorry, I didn't mean to scare you," the newcomer said with a strange accent. He was lean and looked to be in his fifties. His face was strong and kind, but his eyes held mischief. Normally Liam would have made an immediate assessment, especially with eyes like that, but there was an ease in his manner that Liam couldn't remember encountering in anyone except Peter.

He was compelled to engage with this man and try to unravel the mystery. "I was lost in thought."

"My name's Rufus."

"Liam."

Rufus nodded, then focused back out the window. "All these people coming and going for different reasons. Some running. Some returning. Which one are you?"

Liam put his hand in his pocket and wrapped his fingers around the pendant. Just in case. In Liam's experience, these types of conversations were exclusively for assessing a person and then distracting them. If he didn't know better, he'd say this guy was sent by Kyle to steal the pendant. But he couldn't shake the kindness that radiated from him. "Is there something you want?"

Rufus chuckled. "Running."

"And what about you?"

"Me? I'm searching."

"For what?" Liam asked.

"I'll know it when I find it."

"That sounds like the generic answer of someone who's lost and doesn't want to admit it."

Rufus chuckled again and this time Liam joined him without meaning to. "Here comes another one." He pointed out the window. "Where do you think that one's coming from?"

Liam watched the plane land. "No idea."

"You like flying?"

"If it gets me where I'm going."

"Did you know that San Francisco's International Airport has an airport therapy pig to help passengers who are anxious about flying?"

"That can't be true."

"It is. I've seen her. Name's LiLou."

"Does that mean you're an anxious flyer?"

"No, not me, but I know a few who are. That's how I

met LiLou. Someone I was with needed a bit of comforting."

"Did the pig help?"

"Yes. She did. Animals seem to have an innate ability to ease stress. You have any pets?"

"No, I move around too much."

"I got a dog from an animal shelter once, and boy, was she a bad dog. Chewed up everything and refused to be housebroken."

"The shelter must have given her something to make her behave for your visit."

"Oh no. She was a real piece of work there too. They asked me three times if I was sure I wanted her. They had been about to put her down."

"So why'd you pick her?"

"She was a black Lab."

"And?"

"And I've had black labs before. I know what kind of dogs they should be. I guess I wanted to give her the chance to be that dog."

"That's very noble of you. Don't tell me you're one of those nuts who believes everything and everyone is inherently good."

"Oh no. I've seen enough evil in this world to know that's not true. I guess I could have blamed the dog's nature on being abused, but the fact remained, she was nasty, plain and simple. The only thing that was going to change that was if she trusted me enough to give me a chance to look after her. Show her the dog she could be. The kind I wanted her to be."

"And did she?"

"Don't know yet. Still working on it."

"And when do you quit? When is enough enough?"

"Too late now. I took her in, made a commitment to her. If I give up, then I prove to her that trying is useless."

It was ridiculous to Liam, the relief that washed over him knowing that Rufus wouldn't give up on the dog.

"She's a lucky dog, then. I don't think there are many out there who would give her that chance."

Rufus shook his head. "Only me." He turned to Liam. "No one else has ever or will ever love her like I do. I'll give her as many chances as I can until it's too late."

"I thought you said you'd never give up."

Rufus shrugged. "She won't live forever. But until that time comes, I won't stop trying."

The loudspeaker chimed three times, and an announcement was made for the commencement of boarding.

"There's your flight. I gotta get going anyway. Have a good one. It was nice talking to ya." Rufus was lost in the crowd before Liam could ask how he knew it was Liam's flight that was called.

He still had the pendant fisted in his hand to protect it. But as much as he'd like to explain the encounter away as a sinister one, after that dog story, he wondered if it wasn't the type of thing Mrs. Carson would call a God appointment. He didn't like the idea of comparing himself to Rufus's dog, but he couldn't shake the inclination that God was trying to say something.

He headed back to his gate but stopped in the bathroom on his way past to splash water on his face. It was a meager attempt to clear his head and eased nothing. He knew God had been involved in saving Sophie. It might have cost Liam everything, but that was a small price to pay to have her safe. He could humble himself enough to send up a quick thank-you for her life. But as far as where he stood with God, he wasn't so sure. Emily had given him the chance to make things right. But despite the stranger with the dog, he couldn't be convinced God still wanted him. Or maybe it was that the idea of standing before the Creator was too terrifying to contemplate. Easier to simply accept your guilt and move on then to bare your soul to an all-powerful God who had the power over life and death with no more than a breath.

He focused on people watching to clear his head as he boarded the plane. He was always good at that. And right now, he needed something to focus on that gave him confidence.

When he was settled in his seat, he pulled out the pendant, running his thumb along the edge of it. The dark-blue diamond set at the center of the flower looked bottomless. Even the stale lights in the plane didn't diminish the radiance of the pear-shaped diamond petals that looked as though they carried the dew from the morning. No wonder Emily didn't believe his dad when he said it wasn't worth much. Her craftsman eye would have demanded recognition of its worth. It could have set her up for a lifetime, and yet, it had been more valuable to her around her neck. So what was he doing with it in his hand? She hadn't known what it was for when she gave it to him, only that he needed it.

He tucked the flower away and leaned his head back as the plane lifted into the air. Somehow, God had brought people into his life who demonstrated a small portion of who he was. After this was all over, he owed it to them to at least look at what his life had become and see if another path existed. See if God really hadn't given up on him.

Chapter 22

LIAM PARKED his car as close to the food court entrance of the mall as he could. He had no reason to conceal himself, but took his time exiting his vehicle, making sure he'd taken a careful look around first. He would meet Kyle in half an hour at the table closest to the restrooms. They'd make their exchange, and he'd get Sophie back. Kyle had no reason to double-cross him, but Kyle was not a man he trusted.

Liam nodded to the massive black man who stood near the entrance with his hands clasped in front of him. The man nodded back. Liam had called in a few favors to make sure he had Sophie protected. Two more men he had connections to through his special forces days were sitting at nearby tables. Kyle would notice, but for an exchange like this, it should be expected. He'd have his own men ready. They were like two countries with nuclear weapons. They both knew the fallout wasn't worth it but needed the firepower in order to keep the other in check. The only difference was that

Kyle enjoyed the display of power. For Liam, it was only out of necessity.

It was just past ten in the morning, so the food court was quiet. Most of the tables were empty, so Liam picked the one that gave him the best vantage point. He waited, scanning everyone who entered and exited from every direction.

A small child screamed, drawing Liam's attention to McDonalds on the far side of the room. Then his eyes shifted to an older couple sitting close to the door. They started laughing at something in the newspaper they were sharing.

He continued perusing the room, and his back straightened when he saw a group approaching the doors.

Sophie entered first, wearing an oversized coat that she had wrapped tightly around herself. Kyle walked a step behind with two other men following on either side and a smaller man bringing up the rear. When they passed Liam's guy at the door, they made no show of noticing him.

Liam looked over his shoulder and saw what he expected. Two more of Kyle's men stood guard over the path into the rest of the mall.

Kyle smiled broadly and waved as he approached. And after instructing Sophie to stand behind his seat, he sat across from Liam.

"I see you brought company," Kyle said, as if this were a casual meeting of old friends. "I've brought my own. I hope you don't have illusions of grandeur. Just give me what I want and you can have the girl."

Liam saw Sophie's eyes lift to him, tears falling down to her chin.

Liam pulled a small pouch from his pocket and slid it across the table, then he reached a hand out toward Sophie, but Kyle put a hand out to stop Sophie. "One moment, if you please. There's no need to rush. We can all be civilized."

He opened the pouch, smiled, then snapped his fingers to the smaller man who had been fidgeting between the two others who had come in with Kyle.

The man rushed over and sat down, pulling out a loupe to inspect the jewelry.

"Beautiful," he said as he inspected each segment. "Absolutely stunning."

Liam tapped an impatient finger on the cold metal table.

Finally, the jeweler finished his examination. He nodded and handed the pendant back to Kyle before exiting the table.

"Very good. Overall, I'd say that was pretty painless, wouldn't you?"

"No. I wouldn't."

"Maybe you're too uptight. Either way, it was nice doing business with you, Liam." He stood and took Sophie's hand, lifting it. "It has been delightful getting to know you, young lady." He kissed her hand. If she hadn't been terrified, she would have yanked it away and slapped him.

As soon as Kyle let go, she ran to Liam, curling her face into him to hide from the horror she'd been through. "You're safe now," he whispered into her hair.

"Lovely girl. If I didn't already have another to take her place, I might be sad to let her go."

Liam's jaw flexed against his cheek. He couldn't think about Kyle continuing his business right now. He had to get Sophie home. "We're leaving."

"Have a nice life, Liam. And you remember what I said. If you ever get mixed up in my business again, I'll kill you."

"Same goes for you." He pulled Sophie toward the door, keeping his arm around her.

When they got in the car, he rang his sister. "I've got her, Claire. She's safe with me now." He couldn't understand her response through the choking sobs.

Sophie reached for the phone.

He handed it to her and held his breath.

"Oh, Mom." They were both crying now. Liam yelled loud enough so his voice would reach through to Claire. "We're coming home now. We'll see you in about forty."

He started the car and pulled out onto the road as Sophie recounted to her mom parts of the ordeal. It sounded like Kyle had done little to her besides hitting her so her face was bruised. It was for the show. So he could send a video to Liam to make his point. But it was like Liam had said to his sister, Kyle didn't do anything that would compromise him getting what he wanted. That would have changed if Liam hadn't been able to get him the pendant.

"Uncle Liam?"

He had been lost in thought and didn't realize she was off the phone. "Yeah?"

"He said he had another girl to take my place. Do you think that's true?"

He pushed a slim stream of breath between his lips. "It's what he does."

"Can you do something to stop him?"

"Maybe if there was no one I cared about."

"Because he could take me again."

"You or your mom." *Or Emily.* "I can't risk it."

"What about the police?"

"Maybe."

"You don't think they could stop him?"

"I don't know. He's a smart guy. He's careful."

She was quiet for a long time, then said, "Thank you."

"For what?"

"Saving me."

"Don't thank me. Please. I'm the one who got you into this mess."

She wrapped her arms around herself. "He told me."

"Kyle?"

"Yeah, he told me how you saved those other girls, and that's how he knew you would give anything to save me."

"And he was right."

"You're a good man, Uncle Liam. My dad doesn't think so, but I know."

"Doing one good thing doesn't make up for all the bad."

"It does for me."

Liam nodded and let it drop.

Brian was standing at the front door when Liam pulled up. He turned toward the house, and when he faced outside again, Claire came rushing out past him.

Sophie jumped from the car and ran up as Claire met her in the yard. Brian slowly joined them, keeping an eye on Liam as he went. He put his arms around them both, letting his tears fall freely.

Liam remained by his car, waiting for the reunion and the emotions to settle. This wasn't a situation he could talk himself out of and he only stayed because he wanted to give Brian the opportunity to say his piece, no matter how painful it was for Liam. He owed Brian that after everything he'd put that family through.

Sophie was the first to draw attention to him. "Uncle Liam." She turned to go to him, but Brian grabbed her. "No, Soph."

He approached Liam instead. "You can go now."

Liam nodded. "Brian, I know — "

"You know nothing. I don't want you to have anything to do with this family again. Do you hear me?"

"Yeah, I got it."

"Daddy." Sophie ran over. "Daddy, don't do this. It wasn't Liam's fault."

"Yes, it was!" Brian roared. "I'm sorry." He pulled Sophie close. "I'm sorry. I don't mean to yell. You've been through so much. But he has to take responsibility for his actions. He can't expect — "

"But it was only because he was trying to help people."

"Soph, you need to stay out of this, honey. You've been through a serious trauma. You don't need to worry yourself, okay?"

"But I do. That's what I'm saying. At least Uncle Liam tried to do some good."

"But he didn't, did he? All he did was get you in trouble. You want some good done? I can do what Liam couldn't. I'm going to ring the police and we're going to get this guy put in prison."

"Brian." Liam's warning tone got a glare from him. "Going to the police with this is your choice, but you need to be prepared. Kyle will make your life hell in order to get you to back down. You need to make sure you're prepared for that."

Brian closed in on Liam so the rest of his family couldn't hear. "If you try to give me one more piece of advice as a criminal, I will not hesitate to call the police and report you. Or do I need to worry about you threatening my family?"

Liam didn't say another word, but as he drove away, his heart felt as though it had been ripped out and torn into a million pieces that could never be put back together again.

His thoughts jumped to Peter, the one who always seemed to call him home, even when they hadn't spoken in years. The one who knew enough of his secrets to know Liam wasn't worth saving, and yet he still tried. He could have been the stranger at the airport with a story about a stray he was trying to save.

Liam spent the next several days numbly wandering around the city. There had been plenty of times he'd drowned his sorrows in a bottle like the best of them. But he kept finding himself in unexpected places, like sitting on the bank of a river for hours, just staring. Often thinking about Emily.

He wanted to tell her how everything had worked out, that Sophie was safe. Then he convinced himself that it was closure he needed in order to move forward in life and not just a desire to see her again. He had to go back and get his bike. Then he could stop by Oakridge and tell Emily what had happened. Then he could say goodbye. Maybe then he'd have some peace. Maybe.

Chapter 23

ARRIVING BACK in Oakridge was a touch surreal. It had only been a few days, but it felt like a lifetime ago. He'd picked up his bike at the airport and knew it wouldn't be long before the whole town knew he was back. But he wouldn't be there long enough to give them any gossip.

When he saw Stevie come out of the post office, he couldn't help but stop.

"Hey, Liam. I didn't expect to see you back here so soon. I'd heard you left town. I thought it was a more permanent thing."

"It is. I'm not staying long."

"Just long enough to say goodbye?"

Liam smiled. "You must be a good cop."

Stevie shrugged. "I do what I can. Hey, I didn't see you after that incident at the grocery store. That was some good work you did there."

"You would have done the same thing if you were there."

"I read your statement. I don't know that I have your finesse."

"Then I'm glad I could help. Hey, can you do something for me?"

"Yeah, sure."

"Can you keep an eye on Emily? Make sure she's okay?"

"Well, I'll be."

"What?"

"You guys did have something going on."

"Not really. But I got to know her enough to know she's a special girl."

"Did you hurt her?"

Liam rubbed his finger across his bottom lip. "Yeah, I did."

"I'd break your nose, but it looks like you're in more pain than I could ever inflict on you. Yeah. I'll look out for her."

Liam clapped his hand on Stevie's shoulder. "Thanks. I'll see you around."

When he pulled up at Emily's house, he saw her truck was there, but it took him several minutes to get up the courage to go to her door.

After ringing the bell and knocking, to no avail, he went to the main house and tried there, but there was still no answer. He sat on the porch swing for a minute. His knee bounced out the tempo of his pulse. He'd never been so anxious about saying goodbye to anyone before. Even with Claire and Soph, it was awful, but he wasn't edgy like he was now.

He noticed Sam's car was missing. Emily must have gotten a lift into the restaurant. The neighborhood was quiet, but his presence would have been noted. Better not to sit for too long.

He got back on his bike and headed for Maple Leaf. It would be an easier place to say goodbye. All those people meant they'd both have to remain civilized and unemotional.

When he pulled into the full parking lot, he knew she'd be busy, so it would be a quick and painless goodbye. No big deal.

He marched up the line that extended to the parking lot, getting a few glares from people as he squeezed himself through to the door.

This was good. He was in control. He could do this.

"I'm not staying," he said to an older gentleman who attempted to block his entry. "I'm just here to see someone."

Patty greeted him when he walked through the door. "Oh, Liam, hi. I mean, I'm Patty. We haven't met yet, but I heard about you. And I've seen you. I mean, when I was in the store the other day, my friend Sarah pointed you out." The woman was unashamedly flustered. "You know, from the thing where you saved Emily?"

"Uh, okay. I'm actually looking for her, if you can point me in the right direction?"

"Oh. She's not here. I mean, she's supposed to be. She was supposed to come in this morning, but she hasn't turned up yet."

Liam ignored the man behind him, who cleared his throat in annoyance. He was too distracted by the unease that seeped into his belly. "Is that normal for her?" He kept his voice casual. It wouldn't help to alarm anyone.

"Sometimes she works from home. So she might be there. Otherwise, Sam's in the kitchen if you want to ask him. He would know way more than me."

"Great. So I can just go back there?"

"Yeah, sure."

Liam found Sam but was concerned by the look Sam gave him. With a crooked finger, he indicated for Liam to follow.

When he stopped out the back of the restaurant, Liam wondered if he intended to murder him.

"I hope you've come back to apologize." Sam crossed his arms.

Liam leaned against the siding and lowered his head. "She's hurting."

"I don't really know, actually. She won't talk to me. All I do know is she's very sad, not the kind of sad that a girl gets from being dumped, but a deeper grief that changes you. All I could get out of her was that you left town. So I don't know what you did, but you better be here to fix it, or else leave us in peace. Or what's left of it."

"I would like to apologize. If there is anything I can do to make it right, I will. I just need to find her."

"You're going to have to work for it. I haven't even been able to get her out of her house this morning."

"So you've spoken to her?"

"No. She wouldn't even come to the door."

"But she's there?"

"Yeah. Truck's there. She wouldn't have gone anywhere without it."

"Listen Sam, I never meant to hurt her like that. I'll talk to her."

When he got back out to his bike, he rested his hands on top of his head, thinking. It was possible she was avoiding him, but the way they left things, that didn't make sense. If Sam was right and she wasn't leaving her place, it had to do with more than him leaving. He was certain she had wanted him to save Sophie. They had both exposed their deepest secrets. That's not easy to get over. Most likely, she was struggling to process it. It was worth one more check at her place.

He thumped his fist on her door. "Emily? Emily, it's Liam." He looked through the window and knocked on the pane. "Emily. If you're in there, I'm not leaving until you come to the door. I wanted to tell you about Sophie." He waited, but there was nothing from inside the house.

"I don't think she's home," a man called to him from the sidewalk across the road.

Of course, a small town. If he wanted to find out what was happening, ask the neighbor.

Liam jogged over. "Hey, my name's Liam."

"I know who you are."

Liam couldn't tell whether he meant that as a good or a bad thing. This guy had a remarkable poker face. He'd play it safe. "I'm heading out of town. I wanted to say goodbye."

"And we haven't even said hello." The guy looked angry, but then cracked a grin, followed by a bellowing laugh. He punched Liam in the arm. "I'm just messin' with ya. I hear you did good work over at the grocery store. Good to have a guy around town who can handle himself. I'm Fred. I knew your dad a little. Richard was a good guy."

"Yeah. He was a great dad."

"Mm, may he rest in peace. You doing okay?"

"It's hard some days, but I manage. So, about Emily, you said you don't think she's home, but her truck's there."

"Yeah, she left last night with some guy in a fancy car."

"Fancy car?"

"Yeah. I didn't think Emily was into that sort, but sometimes you don't know people. Did you know she moved to the city for a while but then came home?"

"Yeah, I did. Can you remember if Sam was home at the time?"

"Nah, didn't see his car in the driveway."

"Do you remember what kind of car it was that Emily left in?"

"One of those muscle cars. A, um, whatchamacallit. A Mustang, I think it was, or some such."

"Was it blue?"

"Uh, yeah, it looked kinda green, but it was under the yellow streetlight. Could tell it had a real nice metallic paint job, though. You know the fella?"

"I do. Thanks for your help."

Liam raced back to his bike in a panic as Kyle's words rang in his head about having found a replacement for Sophie. His mind went blank as he gripped the handlebars with white knuckles. He'd made a mess of everything. He bashed the heel of his hands against the bar, then grabbed it again as tight as he could.

He couldn't go up against Kyle. Not the way he needed to if he was going to get Emily back alive. He didn't have the manpower for something like that. But it wasn't the sort of thing he could call in favors for.

He took a few deep breaths to steady his breathing and then he did something he thought he'd never do again.

Jesus, I need your help.

Liam rode toward New York City, unsure where he was going or what he would do when he got there, but he wasn't expecting the peace that had settled over him. He had done nothing in his life that deserved God's help and yet, now that he'd cried out to him, he was surprised to find that it felt as though God was willing to give it to him.

He had no plan, not even the makings of one. He had no idea whether Emily would be held in the city here or taken back to Charlotte. But there was one very strong inclination that he wouldn't ignore.

Before entering the city, he pulled over at a truck stop and made a call.

"This is Peter Black."

"Peter, it's Liam."

"Liam. How are you?" His words were stiff.

"I'm okay, but I need your help."

"Are you safe?"

"You've been worried I'm not?"

"Jemi and I haven't stopped praying for you since you left. We thought — Anyway, I'm glad you're safe."

Liam ran a hand down his pants leg. "Thanks, Peter. I mean, for praying. I can tell you it's helped a lot."

"So you were in trouble, then?"

"It's a long story, and while I am safe, there is someone else who isn't, and I need your help. I know I don't deserve it, but — "

"Liam, save your deprivation for another time, and tell me what I can do."

"I'll fill you in on the details later, but the bottom line is that a very dangerous man has kidnapped a friend of mine and I need to get her back."

"Where is he holding her?"

"That's part of the problem. I'm in New York and he has contacts in the city, but he's based in Charlotte, but I have no idea where he'd take her."

"What's your gut say?"

"I don't think he'd bother bringing her back to NC"

"That's what I thought. Too risky. But we'll find her. I know exactly who to call. You send me the names of the parties and vehicle license plates involved if you have any, and I'll get my best onto it. You know that job in New York we talked about when you were here? The one with Oliver?"

"Yeah."

"His wife is the best computer hacker I've ever come across. I'll get her onto it."

"Great."

"You don't happen to know the car she was taken in?"

"I do."

"Perfect. I'll get in touch with Oli and Morgan, and if you head that way, they can either get you on a plane, or you can sit tight and wait for my arrival."

"I don't think sitting is something I'm prepared to do. I've got to get her back."

"Liam, God is in this. He's been in this the whole time. We can trust him."

"I'm doing my best."

Chapter 24

KYLE PUSHED Emily into the room and nodded to a chair in the corner. She wanted to be defiant but didn't want to disrupt the calmness that sat on her. She knew where it came from but didn't know how delicate it was, and she didn't want to lose the odd strength it gave her to be patient and restrained.

When Kyle had turned up at her home with a gun, she had been overcome with a chilling fear that sapped her strength and meant she could do nothing but follow his orders to get into the car.

But the terror that first fell on her was only a memory now. Somehow, as they'd driven into the city, the peace she'd been searching for the past several years finally descended on her. And any time her thoughts angled into the direction of the nightmare that most likely lay ahead for her, God protected her mind. Any other explanation fell short, so now the only thing she could do was trust him.

She sat in the chair, the thump of the heavy bass

from the nightclub above rumbling through her bones. The room smelled like stale liquor, and because she hadn't eaten in a while, it turned her stomach.

Kyle made a phone call. He stood at the other side of the room with his back to her. Odd that he didn't expect her to try to escape, but then his head turned slightly, enough that he could catch sight of her in his peripheral vision. He put his hand on his hip, pushing his jacket back and exposing his gun.

"Right. Get it set up then. I need this done quickly." He hung up and looked at her. "Drink?"

She shook her head, but he poured her one anyway. When he handed it to her, she took it and set it on the floor. "I'm not thirsty."

"Not thirsty? Or don't trust me?"

She stared at her hands, repeating the name Jesus over and over in her head. In this evil place, it was a small light that kept the darkness at bay.

"It's only a drink. I promise."

"I'm not thirsty."

He squatted down in front of her. "You're different than I remember you. I know it's been a few years, but after what you went through, I actually expected you'd have a bit more fight in you. But you really are damaged goods, aren't you? Did I break you last time? Is that what happened?"

She pushed her shoulders back and looked him in the eye. "You think too highly of yourself."

He chuckled. "I'm enjoying this. Are you enjoying this? No, why would you be? I know I'm the only one who will come out of this a winner. But I would like to help." He nodded down at the drink. "It will be worse for you if you don't use anything to dull the pain. That's just whiskey, but I could give you something stronger if you like."

She hated how confident he was. If she knew she could punch the smile off his face and get away with it, she would have. "I don't want anything from you."

"Suit yourself." He stood and paced the room. "Isn't it funny how we find ourselves in the exact same place as before? I mean, this isn't literally the exact same place, but you know what I mean. It's like it's fate or something."

"You can't call it fate if I don't have a choice."

"But you've gotta admit, you coming to Liam's house when I was there … I mean, Liam's dad bought a house in the town you live in? What are the chances?"

"Coincidence doesn't give you the right to kidnap me."

"Nothing gives me the right to kidnap you, but I'm the kind of guy who takes what he wants. And when I saw you the other night, I couldn't stop thinking about you. Thinking about what you did. The gun in your hands." He laughed. "I'm going to make sure *that* doesn't happen again. You left a big mess I had to clean up. And then when the police came for me … " He threw his arms up in the air.

"How'd I get a gun?"

Kyle laughed lightly. "I have no idea. You were so drugged up, I don't even know how you shot anyone. I'm just glad it wasn't me. It was strange, actually. You were falling over yourself, but as soon as you got that gun, you went steady. Then you had to make it through a bunch of corridors to get out onto the street. I came after you and almost had you, but the cops got to you first. Lucky girl. Or not so lucky. You and Liam actually make a great pair. You both are such a hassle to my business."

"Is that why you're going to sell me off? Because I made life difficult for you years ago? Do you know what you did to my life? If you weren't so full of yourself, maybe things wouldn't be so difficult for you, you poor little baby."

"Ohh, there we go. You do have a little fight in you. Nice. I'll get Freddy to add that to the list of your assets. I've got a couple of guys coming who like that."

"You're a pig."

"Maybe, but I'm also a businessman like any other. I sell what's in demand to make money."

"You said yourself I'm damaged goods. Why diminish your reputation by selling an inferior product? Why not let me go?"

"That's a fair enough request." She looked up at him. "I won't, but you can ask it. It's true, I don't think you'll make me as much money as you would have back then. Especially since I'm in a hurry to offload you." He sighed. "Back then, you had this innocence about you that was adorable. Do you know how much people will pay for adorable? I'm glad to see you still have the freckles, but even so, you're harder now than you used to be."

She strained her mind, trying to come up with an argument that would convince Kyle to let her go. There had to be something. *God, please, there has to be something.*

"This is your last chance." She didn't know why she said it, it was just the first thing that came to her.

"What did you say?"

It had touched a nerve, although she had no idea why. "I said, this is your last chance to turn things around. You don't have to do this."

He leaned in close to her face. "I absolutely do have to do it and I'm going to enjoy every. Last. Second."

He winked at her, then reached down to pick up her untouched drink.

She held her breath and jerked up her knee before considering the consequences. Her leg smashed into his face, and he cried out before he fell to the side, the glass shattering on the floor. He was up before she could move and he hit her across the side of the face, sending her sprawling onto the floor. He fell on top of her and punched her in the side, pushing all the wind from her lungs.

Blood fell from Kyle's injured face onto hers. "You don't want me as your enemy in this. You want to live in hell? I can put you there. I can make this as hard for you as you like. So it's your choice how we move forward. We do this the easy way or the hard way. Which do you want?"

He held her down, dripping blood on her and waiting for her answer. "What'll it be?" he screamed into her face and lifted his fist, waiting for her response.

She didn't want to say it. Didn't want to give in, but she finally squeaked out, "Easy."

He pushed off of her and wiped his arm across his

face. "Clean yourself up," he said, then staggered out the door.

Emily stayed where she was, her tears soaking into the concrete floor. She was unsure which pain was worse, the one in her face or her stomach. It hurt to breathe. *God, please help. Please get me out of this. Please.*

Chapter 25

LIAM ENTERED the foyer of a multistory apartment building he had been in two years previously. It looked the same but felt less impressive. Maybe because he was familiar with it now.

"Liam, it's good to see you again," said the man who greeted him as soon as he entered.

"Roger, is it?"

"It is."

"I'm surprised you remember me. It's been a couple of years."

"I never forget a face. And we've been expecting you. If you'd like to follow me?"

Liam entered the elevator with the man he knew to be Oliver Wright's doorman, among other things. Last time he was here, it was under what he considered to be duress. Peter called in a favor and Liam was hesitant to accept, but in the end, it had been a good experience. And now that he needed help himself, he found it amazing how the tables had turned. He remembered

Oliver being a nice guy and hoped he wasn't as reluctant as Liam was about helping.

The first time they met, Liam had thought Oliver was a stuck-up and naïve business owner. But it didn't take him long to appreciate the man was more than he appeared. Even his wife, Morgan, had unknown depths. He'd only heard bits and pieces from Peter originally, but he knew that if he had Oliver and Morgan on his side, he had more help than he'd ever dreamed was possible.

The two men stepped off the elevator and Liam noted the plush gray carpet in the small hallway of the penthouse suite.

"This way," Roger said, heading for the closest door.

He rapped his knuckles twice before opening the door to reveal a room full of computer monitors and other surveillance paraphernalia.

Oliver had been focused on one of the screens but turned at their entrance. A woman sat at a computer but remained focused on her task. He had only met Morgan briefly before.

"Liam." Oliver approached. "Hey. It's good to see you again."

"Likewise." Liam gave Oliver's hand a firm shake. "I really appreciate this."

"I'm glad to return the favor."

"I don't think I did much. I mean, Peter told me it all worked out, but I don't know how much of that was due to my help."

"It would have helped more if I'd listened to you. Peter said you had a gift for reading people."

"I'm pretty sure what I told you was that everyone had question marks over them. But I wasn't sure if any of them would cross the line into murder."

"I didn't need you to point a finger directly. What you did was help me focus. I wanted to see everyone at my company as being on my side. You kind of shattered that expectation. The fact that I didn't want to believe it almost cost Morgan and me our lives."

"I know from personal experience that we can often be our own worst enemy."

"Got him," Morgan said, before jumping up to face the other two.

"Morgan. It's good to see you again."

She brushed her short red hair away from her face before walking over. She took Liam's hand in both of hers and squeezed gently. "Nice to see you, too, Liam. You've got perfect timing. I followed your Mustang to a nightclub in the Bronx."

"Did they stop anywhere on the way? Could he have left her somewhere else?"

"No. Judging by the time, they went straight from Oakridge to the Bronx."

Liam put his hands on his hips and dropped his head. "When does Peter arrive?"

"Tonight," Oliver said. "We already booked the flight in case he needed to come up, and it looks like that's what's happening."

"Okay. I can't stay here till then. I'll go crazy, so if you can grab me the address, I'll head down there and keep an eye on the place. Then we can regroup when Peter arrives."

"I'll come with you," Oliver said, grabbing his coat off the back of a nearby chair.

"Hang on a sec," Morgan said.

"We need you here," Oliver said, yanking his coat over his shoulders.

"I'm not offering to come, but I'd like to know if there is any more I can do on this end. Is there anywhere else I can look into? I can check cell phones or email chatter."

Liam thought for a minute. "I can give you the number I have for Kyle, but most of his work stuff goes through burners. And check for anything to do with that nightclub. I'd be surprised if you find anything, but it's worth looking at. Most of what you'd find would be in code, so you might end up with a lot to sift through."

"If I find anything that looks promising, I'll let you know. And I'll watch for any movement at the club from here. I've got a new facial recognition program I'm keen to try out, so I should be able to get you names of people who are coming or going."

Liam slapped Oliver on the arm. "Where'd you find her?"

He grinned. "She found me."

"Saved his life. More than once, actually."

"That's a pretty good track record."

She shrugged. "I do what I can. Now, I'm going to get back to work. You guys be careful."

The two men sat in silence after Oliver parked his car across the street from the nightclub. A tree-lined island in the middle of the road offered a small amount of cover, but since it was the middle of the day, there was no movement besides passing pedestrians. And with all the traffic coming and going, they wouldn't be noticed.

Oliver unbuckled his seat belt and crossed his arms, trying to get comfortable. "So this woman we're looking for, she family?"

Liam kept his eyes focused on the building across the road. "No."

"But she's important to you."

"She's a friend."

"It's just, Morgan's life was in danger once."

"You said you two almost lost your lives."

"Yeah. I don't know if Peter told you. We went to Libya and were kidnapped. Morgan was a smart girl who wanted to help me find out who was trying to kill me. I told myself she didn't matter to me beyond that." He let out a pop of breath. "It took me a while to admit to myself that I cared a lot more about her than I wanted to. I would have done anything to save her."

"I'm not sure what your point is. This isn't the same as that. I haven't known Emily for very long."

"I didn't know Morgan for very long. But guys our age, we've been around long enough. We've known enough women that it doesn't take long to recognize someone who's different."

Liam didn't like where Oliver was going with this. He always did his job best when he kept emotion out of it. That's what went wrong on the job with Emily, and he couldn't afford to make the mistake again. "And?"

"And I'd like to understand what level of commitment you're putting into this. If you're approaching this like any other mission, I get that, but if this is personal, I'd like to know that too."

Liam stared at the door to the club. He would storm through that door right now if he thought it would save her. Try all he wanted, he couldn't remove the emotion from this job. Just like Oliver, he'd do whatever it took to save Emily, and Oliver was putting himself on the line to help, so he had a right to know. "It's personal."

"Okay. Then I'll fight to get her back like I would for Morgan."

"I can't ask you to do that."

"You didn't ask."

"I was honest with you because I wanted you to know the risks of working with a man who might not have his emotions under control."

"You think your emotional attachment to Emily makes this job more dangerous?"

"I know it does."

"Interesting theory."

"Born out of a great deal of experience."

"And probably true."

"It is true."

"Except in this case."

"I don't follow."

"Liam, none of this is random. God's in this whether or not you want to admit it."

"I know."

"Oh, that was not the response I expected."

"I can only imagine the things Peter said to you, but I will admit, in desperation, I cried out to God for help, and judging by how things are unfolding, I'd say he's responded. But that doesn't mean I just toss all my training and experience out the window."

"No, it doesn't. But if your connection to Emily makes things harder, you can't change that and God can cover it. None of us gets it right all the time, but if he's willing to help, then you need to accept it."

A blue Mustang pulled out onto the street from behind the nightclub. Both men's attention was immediately diverted.

"I can only see a driver, no passengers. Do we follow?" Oliver asked, pulling out his phone.

"No. I stay where Emily is."

Oliver made a phone call on speaker. "You catch that?" he asked when Morgan answered.

"I'm on it."

"We couldn't see a passenger, but that doesn't mean there isn't one. We're staying put but let us know if you spot anything and keep us updated on his movements."

"I know the drill."

"One other thing. Can you access the blueprints for this building? I think we'll need to enter it at some point tonight."

"Already on it."

"'Course you are."

"Hey." Morgan's voice softened. "You think you'll be home tonight? 'Cause I was thinking about — "

"You're on speaker," Oliver interrupted.

Liam turned his face toward the window to hide his smile, and Morgan cleared her throat. "I was going to say, I was thinking of ordering takeout."

"Yeah, sounds good. Let's do that. I can grab something on my way home if things here don't go too late."

"Right. Oh! hang on. I found your Mustang at a gas station. Looks like your guy is using a pay phone. I'll stay on him."

"Great, keep us posted."

"She's sharp," Liam said after Oliver hung up. "Is there anything she can't do?"

"She's not much of a cook, but her other skills more than make up for that."

"Is that so?" Liam raised an eyebrow.

"With computers." Oliver's face reddened and Liam chuckled.

"I take it married life is suiting you just fine."

"What can I say? I love my wife."

Chapter 26

THERE WAS NO MORE movement all day except Kyle returning to the club after dark. Morgan had updated them on his whereabouts, which included stopping at a convenience store for supplies.

Not long after Kyle returned, Peter met them on the street after catching a cab. He slipped into the back of the car, followed by another man, a little younger than the rest.

"Solomon?" Oliver said.

"Hey, Oli, it's good to see you again."

"Peter, you didn't say Solomon was coming." Oliver reached into the back to give the new arrival a companionable slap.

"I wasn't sure he'd be able to make it until I arrived at the airport. I thought we could use a fourth here."

"Uh, I don't think we've met," Liam said, holding out his hand to the newcomer.

Solomon shook his hand and Peter explained. "Liam, you remember I told you about one of the women who was saved when Jemi and I met? The one who was pregnant?"

"Yeah, sure. So this is him. Man, Solomon, it is a real pleasure to meet you."

"Glad I can help. So where are we up to? What's the story?"

"You two see the blueprints I forwarded?" Oliver asked.

"Yeah. We had a close look on the way over."

"Thoughts?"

"They have a basement, so that's going to be the most likely place they'd be keeping her. But after looking through their website, I see they have an upstairs VIP section that can be accessed privately, so if there is a meeting taking place tonight, that would be our best shot."

"We've been monitoring all the patrons," Liam said. "So far, no one stands out. But Morgan said there have been a couple of guys who have kept their faces hidden from the camera. I'd say Kyle knows about it and would have given the VIPs a heads-up."

Peter pulled his gun from the holster and handed it forward. "Tuck that somewhere safe."

Solomon followed suit. "I'm getting in on this action. I've been sitting around too long."

"You two plan on going somewhere?" Oliver asked before stowing the two guns in the glove box.

"We're going inside. Have a look around."

"I'll go with you," Liam said.

"Too risky," Peter said. "If Kyle sees you, we'll lose

our chance. Besides, Solomon's good. He's done a lot of undercover work."

"I can't keep sitting here."

"Sure you can. You're a trained professional."

"But if you see Emily in there — "

"If we have the chance to save her now, we'll take it, but that means we need you out here ready to back us up. Come on, Liam, if you think you're going inside now, you're obviously not thinking straight. You should know that's a bad idea. And don't forget, I'm not completely worthless. I do know a thing or two about this sort of stuff."

"Fine, but I don't like it." Liam crossed his arms, resigned to his fate.

"You're going to feel awful until this is over with. But that's why we're here, to help you get through it and to save Emily. We won't be long." Peter jumped out of the car before Liam could protest further.

Solomon didn't say a word, just lifted his eyebrows at Oliver before exiting.

Liam and Oliver watched them cross the street and get in line.

"Don't worry about them," Oliver said.

"I'm not worried about them. I just don't like other people putting themselves in harm's way for my mistakes."

"Would you rather we left you to your own devices?" Liam didn't bother responding. "Then stop sulking and get on board with the rest of us."

"You want to know the last job I did? Saving my niece from the same man who has Emily. I thought when I gave him what he wanted, everything could go back to the way it was."

"You were happy the way things were?"

"It was better than now."

"So, this guy must really have it in for you."

"I don't know. I don't know why he took Emily. It doesn't make sense. He wanted nothing more to do with me either. So why do this?"

"The usual motivators are power or money, but it sounds like this is personal. How'd you get mixed up with him, anyway? Has he always been your enemy, or is there more to that story?"

"Kyle and I used to be friends and we worked together for a time." Liam looked at him sideways. "Small stuff. We were a couple of stupid kids. But then Kyle got hurt by something I did and — I don't know. Maybe he's just doing it to hurt me back."

"That's rough. But regret never helped anyone."

"Are you saying you never did anything you regretted that's followed you around your whole life?"

"I've had regrets. Almost ruined my chance at a relationship with Morgan. But there's no point letting God in if you're not going to let him take away all your sin. You don't get to pick and choose which ones you deserve to be forgiven for. He took them all. Anything less and you've destroyed the power of the cross."

"You make it sound simple. It's not simple."

Oliver laughed. "Someday I'll tell you about my childhood."

"Last time we met, you told me your dad left you for dead."

"Yeah. I was abducted and tortured, but I'd rather not get into it at a time like this."

"But you survived."

"From the circumstances, yeah, but it followed me around for a while and I made some pretty poor choices that caused a lot of people to get hurt. Including myself."

"So what did you do? I can't run away from the stuff I've done."

"Then don't."

"Right, so I should walk into the police station and confess."

"You know Peter would support you. I'd support you."

Liam shook his head. "Not a simple decision to purposely give up your freedom."

"See, that's the mistake you're making. You think that right now you're free? Taking responsibility for what you've done will probably get you locked up for a while, but you'd be free on the inside and that's something you've never had. I think deep down, it's what you want."

The car was silent until Peter and Solomon jogged back across the street.

Solomon glowed when he got in the car. "That was fun."

"You make me feel old," Peter said to him.

"The job I just finished was boring. Required no creativity whatsoever."

"Well, you did good in there. I felt like a proud dad."

"Aw, shucks."

Liam cleared his throat. "So?"

"Right, sorry," Peter said. "So here's the deal. We got a peek in the VIP lounge."

"How'd you manage that?" Liam said.

"Sol wasn't kidding when he said he had fun. You should have seen him."

"It's nothin'. You just tell them what they want to hear," Solomon said.

"Sol, you could charm the flute off a snake charmer."

Solomon laughed. It had an ease to it that indicated he found it easy. "Is that even a saying?"

"I just said it. Anyway, we got a look, and there are four very serious-looking guys in there so far. Not the standard patrons to that particular establishment."

"I got pictures," Solomon said, pulling out his phone. "Punch your number in there and I'll send them to your girl." He handed the phone over to Oliver.

"Done." Oliver handed the phone back and texted Morgan with a quick explanation.

"Hang on a sec," Liam said. "They didn't notice you taking pictures?"

"I caused a distraction," Peter said.

"I guess you were right. You didn't need me in there."

Oliver's phone rang. "It's Morgan." He answered it. "You find something? That was quick."

"Yeah, I'm impressed with this program. None of those guys entered in the front," she said.

"You're sure? You said you didn't get some faces."

"Yeah, but the way they're dressed isn't the same and body shapes don't match up."

"We already know there's an entrance at the back." Liam pinched his bottom lip. "There must be access back there from another street. If we don't get Emily out of there, they'll take her out that way and we'll be too late. If we aren't already."

"Judging by the chatter I've picked up, I'd say she's still there," Morgan said. "Word is, there is a one-night-only bargain. No cover charge."

"We had to pay to get in," Peter said.

"Yeah," Morgan continued, "and I can't find anything about it on social media. They aren't promoting it anywhere. Just some very discreet mentions, I'd say, for those who know where to look for it. I'm confident this is for Emily."

"Great. Thanks, Morgan. I think that confirms for us we need to act now."

Chapter 27

KYLE THREW the door open and tossed a makeup bag at Emily's feet. His eye was black and his nose swollen, but it didn't seem to bother him. "Fix yourself up. You're a mess."

Emily put a hand to her bruised face and pushed the bag away with her toe. She had been continuing to pray nonstop since Kyle left the room and she had felt certain of God's presence with her, but now that Kyle was back in the room, that feeling got hazy.

Kyle put his hand in his jacket pocket. "I'm out of patience, I'm afraid." He pulled out a syringe.

"Wait." Emily grabbed for the makeup. The idea of being drugged dissolved what was left of her calm. "I'll put it on. Just don't drug me."

"I don't know what you have against this stuff. It'll make things easier on you."

"No. No, I don't need the drugs."

He put the needle away. "If you cause me any problems, I won't hesitate to use it."

"I know." She pulled out a compact and looked at the purply marks on her face, dabbing in compliance. She tried hard to trust God, but she didn't know whether his plan was to save her from all of this, or to help her through something she couldn't begin to imagine. Either way, she didn't want to be out of her mind when it happened. At least, she didn't think she did.

Kyle watched her for a minute, then crossed his arms over his chest. "Can I ask you a personal question?"

"Do I have a choice?"

"I'm curious about Liam. What you see in him. I mean. You don't actually think he's been honest with you."

She lowered the makeup. "How do you know? You have no idea what he's told me."

"Don't need to. Not with a guy like that. You're afraid of me, but not of him. But we're the same."

"Liam is nothing like you." She lifted the makeup again so she didn't have to look at him.

"You'd be surprised. We're cut from the same cloth, he and I. Meeting a pretty girl doesn't change that."

"That's got nothing to do with it."

"So you really have fallen for it? He always had a real knack for it. People can't help but believe the lies that pour out of that man's mouth. Even me."

"So it's not me you're getting back at. It's Liam."

He took a step closer. "Liam deserves everything he gets."

"Why, 'cause he went along with your stupid plan all

those years ago and then ran out on you when you got caught? Abandoned you to your fate?"

She didn't see it coming. Light exploded around her when he slapped her across the face. "Don't act like you know anything about it," he yelled. Then he leaned in close. "You said this was my last chance to turn things around. You think that has something to do with Liam?"

Emily waited for her vision to clear before responding. "How should I know?"

He gave her a shove, then stormed out of the room.

She lifted the mirror and looked at the new red welt on her face. Tears blurred her vision. She sniffed them back and closed her eyes to focus on her breathing. It probably would be easier if she were drugged, but the thought of being out of her mind was not one she was willing to consider.

He will cover you with his feathers, and under his wings you will find refuge.

Her eyes sprang open in surprise when the words from Psalm 91:4 floated through her mind. It was a psalm she hadn't thought of for a very long time.

When she had first returned home from the city, the nightmares were unbearable and she'd begun memorizing verses to recite as she fell asleep. Then when she woke in terror, the sheets soaked with sweat, they helped calm her, but this was the first time they reached into the darkest places of her heart to give her strength. Most of the scriptures she hadn't looked at in a long time, having given them up as useless when the nightmares didn't go away.

Her lips moved to recite the verse again. "He will

cover you with his feathers, and under his wings you will find refuge; his faithfulness will be your shield and rampart." Then another one came, another psalm. This time it was from chapter 116:1 (NIV). "I love the LORD, for he heard my voice; he heard my cry for mercy." Her voice trembled. "Because he turned his ear to me, I will call on him as long as I live." Strength blossomed deep within. She lifted the mirror again, continued putting on the makeup, her lips moving as different verses drifted from the recesses of her mind.

When she finished her task, she put the makeup bag aside and sat up straight. She had no idea what was about to happen to her, but there was one thing she was certain about. Her God, the God who created the universe, would be with her every step of the way.

It was only twenty minutes before the door opened. Kyle looked appreciatively at the work she'd done to hide her bruises.

She looked him in the eye and whispered one last prayer. "The Lord is my helper, so I will not fear. What can man do to me?"

"What was that?" he asked, moving closer.

Emily's lip quivered, but her voice was strong. "I said, 'The Lord is my helper, so I will not fear. What can man do to me?'"

Kyle clapped his hands together. "I can't believe it. I never would have guessed you for a Christian. Or are you one of those closet religious folks who went to mass once as a kid? Maybe you were christened? And now that you're in trouble, you think God's going to come rescue you after you've ignored him your whole life. Is that what all that last-chance stuff was about?" Emily saw something that looked like fear flash through his eyes, but he blinked it away. "Father Carl said something similar. I wish you two could meet. He'd get a real kick out of it."

"Father Carl?"

"Yeah, he's my priest. At least he tries to be. Hard to imagine, I know. But believe it or not, there was a time when I hung around the church as a kid. Unfortunately, it didn't do me any good."

"It could if you let it. You haven't run out of chances with God."

Kyle laughed, but it was forced. Then he grabbed a chair and put it in front of her. He sat down with his elbows on his knees. "That's really cute. You're trying to save me. Maybe you still have a thing for me after all?" He reached out his hand and brushed her cheek with his fingers. She yanked her face away. "Or maybe not."

He reached out again and took hold of her chin this time. She tried to yank free, but he held her jaw tight. He moved her head from one side to the other to see the full effect of the makeup job.

"I'd like to meet him," she said after he let go. "Father Carl."

"Maybe you can one day. You two can have a party in heaven if you're the good girl you pretend to be. Or maybe you aren't what you appear to be and one day you and I can hang out in hell. Either way, we still have today, so carpe diem. Party's about to start. Let's go."

"I'm going with you," Liam said.

"Come on, Liam, we've already talked about this. It's not a good idea."

"I'm sorry, Peter, but I can't stay here. Not this round. I'll keep my head down, but even if Kyle sees me, we are there to get Emily out, so it doesn't matter one way or the other."

"Before we get into the specifics of the raiding party," Solomon said, "can I put forward one glaringly obvious problem we have not yet addressed?"

"What's that?" said Peter.

"What about weapons? They're sending everyone through the metal detector, remember?"

"I've got an idea," Oliver said as he retrieved the guns previously deposited in the glove box and handed them back to their owners. "I'll cause a distraction out here. Draw the bouncers out."

"It would have to be pretty sensational. A drunk causing a commotion won't do the trick."

"What about a drunk tossing handfuls of C-notes?"

Peter snorted. "Since when did you start talking gangster?"

"It's this neighborhood. I can't help myself."

"That could work," Liam said. "No one can ignore hundred-dollar bills. But are you sure you can part with the money?"

"I've got plenty."

"Okay, then. Let's go with that."

Solomon laughed. “Man, I’ve been missing out on so much working alone. I can’t wait to see this.”

“I’m getting in line.” Liam got out of the car and Solomon followed.

“Oliver,” Peter said, grabbing his arm before he got out. “After we go in, give us ten minutes, then call the police. We won’t be able to clean up this mess ourselves.”

“What about Liam?”

“Let me worry about him.”

“You got it.” He pulled out his phone to call Morgan. “Good luck in there,” he yelled to Peter, then headed off down the road to collect what he needed. “Hey, babe,” Oliver said when Morgan answered.

“Babe? Are you undercover right now or something?”

“No, I think there’s something in the air down here. Have you got eyes on the front of the club?”

“Yeah, why? Should I be looking for something?”

“Not yet, but you will not want to miss what happens next.”

“Is something about to go down?”

“You could say that. Just make sure you’re tuned in.”

The other three men lined up behind several women, who kept turning to smile at them.

Peter looked down at the sidewalk and mumbled to Liam. “I’ll let you guys deal with this. This is way outside of my area of expertise.”

Liam sucked on his teeth. "I don't know. You seem like a pretty smooth guy to me."

Solomon turned to the other two. "Guys, you are both going to blow our cover. You need to relax." He turned back around and tucked his hands in his pockets. "Good evening, ladies. You're all looking stunning tonight."

A tall redhead spoke first. "You gentlemen are all looking fine yourselves." She winked at Peter, who smiled to hide his surprise. He scratched the back of his head and used the opportunity to turn to Liam. "Oliver better hurry. There is a lot I can do, but I cross the line at flirting with a woman who is not my wife."

"Do you still flirt with your wife?"

"All the time."

"That's actually really nice."

"Hey guys," Solomon said. "How about we buy these ladies a drink once we get inside?"

"Sure thing," Liam said.

Peter tugged Solomon back enough so he could speak without being heard. "What are you doing?"

"Trying not to blow our cover. When Oliver gets back, they'll be chasing after hundred-dollar bills, not thinking about getting a drink with us. But if we stand here like a bunch of stuffed shirts, we'll be noticed."

"He's right, Peter. I, of all people, should know how important appearances are. It's what I do after all." He turned back to the women. "So, you ladies come here often? It's our first time."

"Ooh," said a blonde with a dark-purple dress that

left little to the imagination. "A first-timer. I'd be glad to show you around."

"Yeah, we're new in town," Peter said. Solomon choked on a laugh. "How can you be so good at so many other things?" he said to Peter under his breath.

"Thank goodness. There he is," Peter said when he spotted Oliver appearing from around the corner with a bottle of rum in his hand and his pockets bulging. "This I can do," he whispered, then spoke louder. "Hey, what's up with that guy?"

Everyone turned. Liam's eyes widened. "Not bad. He makes a convincing drunk guy."

Peter sighed. "Finally, we can move on to what I do best."

"Hellloooo — " Oliver belched and stumbled. "My fellow consumers. Howsit goin'?" His gaze lifted to the security camera, and he waved at his wife before reaching into his pocket and flinging out his first fistful of money. Startled gasps came from a few of the waiting patrons before they moved in on him. Solomon snorted a laugh while the three men scooted past the group of women who had caught on to what was happening and headed for the mad rush to gather green.

Oliver staggered into the street and began shouting about the frivolities of life.

"If he uses too many big words, they won't be convinced he's trashed," Peter said, trying not to laugh.

"No, it's perfect," said Liam. "Any toffee-nosed rich guy has got such a command of superfluous language he'd likely overuse it while drunk. Trust me. He's doing a great job of selling it."

More bills rained down from the sky and the crowd took on a fever pitch.

"See you on the other side." Oliver bellowed. The comment was for his friends, but those closing in heard the ramblings of a madman.

The last guard finally moved out toward the commotion.

"You sure know some colorful people," Solomon said to Peter as they slipped through the door.

No one inside was yet aware of what was taking place on the street. The throbbing music and press of bodies made it difficult to move across to the other side of the room where the stairs up to the VIP section were. But it was better than the stampede that would occur if everyone knew about the ATM outside. It also helped the men to remain undetected.

"Wait here," Liam yelled to the other two, and he weaved his way to the bar. He ordered three soft drinks, endured the strange look from the bartender, then brought the drinks back to his friends. "Won't be as obvious if we're standing to the side having a drink."

"Bouncer's new," Peter shouted, taking his drink. "He wasn't there when we were in here earlier."

Liam nodded. "I'd say that means things have begun upstairs." His jaw clenched, and he focused on the sticky floor, clearing his mind of the terrible thoughts that were clamoring for his attention. If he allowed himself to picture what they were doing to Emily right now, he'd move too fast. Peter grabbed his arm and pulled him close.

"Just follow me, okay? Focus on the job, not the people involved."

Liam bobbed his head in a tight nod.

A moment later, the bouncer pressed his earpiece so he could hear better. He stiffened, looked up the stairs, then went for the exit like a bull, pushing people out of his way in the wake.

Peter nodded at the other two and led the way up the stairs.

Chapter 28

EMILY STOOD SILENTLY in the middle of the room with her hands clasped in front of her. Her heart pounded, and the way everyone looked at her, she was sure they must see it. The psalms she tried to keep running through her head began jumbling up, so she fell back to repeating "Jesus" over and over again. She didn't speak out loud, but her lips were moving.

One of the men, a short, bald man with a broad chest and a firm jaw, had a quiet word with Kyle, then approached her. He ran his hand down her arm as he walked around, then pinched some of her hair between his fingers. He looked her in the eyes, then stepped back. "You haven't given her anything?"

"As you can see, she doesn't need it. She's very compliant."

The short man shook his head. "There's something you're not telling us." He turned to the others. "We're all here for a good deal, but I think we deserve to know the cost to us for taking her off your hands. Is someone looking for her?"

Kyle took a deep breath, as if explaining something that should be obvious. He made eye contact with some of the others as if sharing in the joke. "Jacob, I would expect you, of all people, to understand the situations without having to ask such trivial questions." Someone in the room snickered. "If you don't have the capacity to deal with some minor inconveniences, then why have you come?"

Jacob clicked his tongue and stepped back.

"Has everyone had a satisfactory look? Because I'd like to start the bidding."

Emily closed her eyes and tried to slow her breathing. She was lightheaded, but she couldn't afford to pass out. If there was any chance of escape, she needed to be ready for it, no matter how small. God had somehow gotten her free all those years ago, even in her drug induced stupor, and she wanted to be ready if he gave her the opportunity again.

A loud thump at the door brought everyone's attention that way. Kyle's hand went to a gun at his side.

A hand wrapped around Emily's arm. It was the short man. He pulled her toward the door at the back where the others were heading while Kyle was distracted. She tried to pull away, but he had a strong grip. He yanked again and with Kyle as the only one available to save her, she didn't know what to do, but she hesitated long enough that Jacob shoved her hard toward the door and she fell. He attempted to scoop her up when another loud bang splinted the door open.

Jacob left her to make his escape, but the man who broke down the door ran through the room, yelling back to the others who were with him. "Secure the room," he said as he dove through the back door.

Kyle had ignored the man as he charged through the room, and instead, had his gun aimed at the broken door. Emily looked back that way and saw Liam, who had his gun pointed at Kyle. Both men looked like they would shoot.

Emily yelled at them to stop, and Kyle looked her way long enough that Liam jumped for him, grabbing his gun arm and tackling him to the ground.

A shot rang out and Emily screamed.

The third man who entered after Liam had a couple of guys against the wall. He kept his gun pointed at them, but was trying to help Liam, who was wrestling on the ground with Kyle.

Kyle got behind Liam and wrapped his arm around his throat, yanking back hard.

"You don't have to do this." Liam choked out.

"Oh yes, I do. Let's finish this, friend," Kyle growled.

Liam kicked out, loosening Kyle's grip. He threw his elbow back into Kyle's ribs and spun around, grabbing his arm and yanking it backward.

Peter came back in the room with Jacob in tow, who he shoved toward Solomon to take care of as Kyle struggled to get out from under Liam.

Peter pointed the gun. "Enough. It's over, Kyle." Kyle stilled.

Liam looked across at Emily. "You okay? You hurt?" He was out of breath and his lip was bleeding.

"I … I think I'm fine." She wanted to rush to him but wouldn't go near Kyle.

Liam turned his attention back to Kyle. "It didn't have to be this way. If you wanted me out of your life, then why'd you take Emily?"

Kyle smiled. Blood covered his teeth. "I took Emily because it suited me. It never occurred to me you actually cared about anyone but yourself."

Liam shoved into his back. "You're lying."

Kyle laughed. "Am I? Or are you carrying around so much guilt, you can't let me go? Maybe I took her because I wanted to see if you had a soul. When you walked away from me that day, I wasn't so sure."

"I never should have left you. I'm sorry."

Kyle spit blood onto the floor. "You think I'm mad at you for leaving me with that monster? You did me a favor. You showed me what a coward you are."

"You still have a chance, Kyle."

"Oh yeah? You gonna let me go?"

"No, but you can at least face what you've done."

"It's not what I've done, Liam. It's who I am. It's what you are."

"Liam," Peter got his attention. "You and Sol take Emily and get out of here. Let me clean up this mess."

"No. I'm not going anywhere."

"Liam, the police are on their way."

Emily jumped up and made a move toward Liam. "You've got to go. You'll go to prison if you don't get out of here."

"Yeah."

Kyle started laughing and Liam twisted his arm around tighter to shut him up.

Emily reached out a hand to him. "Then let's go."

"We can't keep running from our past, Emily."

"Then I'll stay with you."

"No. I need to face things this way. You don't. I mean, not unless you want to, but they won't need your testimony to make the case. I've got enough on Kyle. You can go home."

"But you'll go to prison."

"Yeah. But I'm ready."

Peter pulled Liam off Kyle, but kept his gun trained. "Don't move. I have no problem shooting you."

Kyle rolled over and sat up against the couch. "I can tell that about you. You'd shoot a man in cold blood. I can see it in your eyes."

"Can't get inside my head. Sorry." Peter lowered his voice to Liam. "Go say goodbye."

Liam took Emily's hand and pulled her into the hall at the back.

"I can visit you," Emily said, squeezing his hand.

"No, don't. Please. The only way I can do this is if I know you've moved on with your life. I need to know you're doing well. Start selling some furniture. Get your life back. Let me be part of your past."

"You say that like your life is over."

"I have to accept that it is. I've got a lot I'm going to have to pay for, but at least that means I won't have to be carrying it anymore. I have to do this."

"I know."

Liam stepped closer. "You've done more for me than you could ever realize."

She brushed the tears out of her eyes. "I'm going to miss you."

"Good." He grinned.

"And thank you for saving me. Again."

"Any time."

Peter stuck his head through the door. "We need to go."

"Give me a sec," Emily said, then she leaned forward and kissed Liam hard on the mouth. He had hoped for a quick, painless goodbye, but now that she was there, he wrapped his arms around her and kissed her back. It was a gift he hadn't expected, and he wanted to take it with him and remember it always.

When they pulled apart, he pinched his lips closed to keep the feel of her as long as he could, then they moved back into the room.

"We've got to go, now," Peter said and shook Liam's hand. "I'll keep in touch."

Liam held the gun out to the group, who were all now gathered on a couch. He nodded at Peter and Sol and his eyes lingered on Emily as they left through the back.

Emily tried not to think as Peter led her down the back stairs, his hand pressed lightly on her back.

"My name is Peter, by the way," he said as he led her out the back door, which came out on a side street.

"Are you the Peter who trained Liam in special forces?"

"Oh, so he told you about me, did he?"

"He did. Thank you for everything you did."

"It was all Liam. He's the one who found out what had happened. We're here for him."

"No, I mean before. For telling him about God. I think it's what saved us all in the end."

They hurried across the street and got in the car as the police poured in through the front door.

"Whoa, you overdid it on the rum," Solomon said, pinching his nose as he slipped into the front seat. Oliver smiled from the driver's seat, looking disheveled but pleased.

"Yeah, sorry. Not much I can do about the smell, but that was the most fun I've had in a long time. So, you're Emily, I take it?"

"Yeah."

"Where's Liam?"

Emily turned to Peter. "Is he going to be okay?"

Peter looked at Oliver. "He's facing his demons."

"Then he'll be great," Oliver said, starting the car.

Peter handed Emily a card. "That's my number on there. If you ever need to talk about this stuff, you call me. I'll keep an eye on Liam. I don't know what the consequences will be, but it's better this way."

"I know. I just didn't want to have to say goodbye. Not after everything that's happened. But thank you, all of you, for what you did to help me tonight. It's good to know Liam has friends who care about him."

"I only just met the guy," Solomon said with a wink.

Peter reached over the seat and shoved his head. "It's

a good thing I know these guys and can vouch for them."

"But who vouches for you?" Solomon laughed.

"Are you ever serious?"

"Not when I can help it."

"Sorry about him. He really loves his job."

Emily smiled. "Don't apologize. It's nice to have someone to lighten the mood. Although I have to ask why it smells like a liquor store in here."

Oliver raised his hand. "My fault."

"Long story," said Peter. "I'll tell you all about it on the drive home."

Emily stood in the shower and held nothing back. After so many years of trying to hold it together, it was the first time she felt safe to fall apart. After seeing what God did for her, she knew she wasn't strong enough to hold it in any longer.

Peter had reminded her of Jesus's words: "Come to me, all of you who are weary and carry heavy burdens, and I will give you rest. Take my yoke upon you … " And that's what she was doing, exchanging her heavy yoke for his light one. She let her tears flow freely until wracking sobs had her curled up in a ball over the drain. Her mind became a black chasm as she allowed the hurt all the space it demanded, and pain exhumed from the deepest parts of herself. She thought she'd forgiven her mom enough a long time ago, but as different memories surfaced, she handed them over as well. She thought of

Kyle and whom he had become because of what had happened to him. Even though she knew nothing about her mom's past, she assumed her abusive behavior came from buried pain. It didn't excuse her for what she did, but it helped Emily come to terms with it. And she knew she would never be free of her own pain if she didn't forgive those who hurt her the most and let God take it from there.

When the tears dried up, she remained on the floor of the shower, overwhelmed and exhausted, but also freer than she'd ever felt before.

She picked herself up when the hot water cooled, but only got as far as wrapping herself in a towel before climbing into bed and falling into a dreamless sleep.

A bird chirping outside the window was the first thing Emily noticed when she awoke, followed by a terrible headache, most likely brought on by all the crying the night before.

She blinked and laid still, aware that the anxiety that usually greeted her in the morning wasn't there. Closing her eyes, she pictured Jesus sitting with her on the bed. She'd tried that same thing so many times in the past, but it was never real. This was the first time she had a deep knowing that he was there with her. That he'd always been there with her, and as much as she was glad not to have to be involved with whatever came next with Kyle, she knew she had the strength to face it if she had to.

She sat up in bed, raked her fingers through her hair,

and decided it was time to stop hiding from life — from the people who mattered the most in her life.

Sam was rocking on the porch swing, his hands wrapped around a mug.

"Hi, Dad."

He jumped up. "Emily, I uh … I've been worried. When you wouldn't answer the door, I was afraid you'd fallen into a deep depression or something. Fred said Liam came looking for you. Said you had left in a car, but I knew that wasn't like you. He must have seen the neighbor or something."

"Yeah. Dad, I've got a lot to tell you, and it won't be easy for you to hear."

"I'm just glad to see you up and about. I don't know what Liam did to you, but it must have been bad."

"No, it wasn't Liam."

"Oh?"

"I didn't answer the door for you because I wasn't there."

"Really? Then where have you been?"

Emily watched her dad as she gave him the barest facts. But he didn't need details to understand how bad it was. His face was red, but the anger that simmered under the surface remained there. Every time he opened his mouth to respond, he stopped himself. His eyebrows remained pushed hard together.

They had both been quiet for a long time while she waited to give her dad time to absorb everything she'd just told him.

Finally, his eyebrows parted. "I wish you would have told me sooner," he said quietly. "I wish Liam wasn't the one who had to come to your rescue."

"I know."

"And after all those years. I knew something was wrong, I just … I can't believe you dealt with all of that on your own. That must have been — " His voice cracked, and he swiped away tears. "I should have known. I should have seen it."

"You did know. You always knew something wasn't right. But it was me. I wouldn't tell you. Besides, you had your own stuff to deal with. You had your life to rebuild after Mom died. To learn how to think for yourself again."

He huffed out a sardonic laugh. "While I rebuilt my life, yours fell apart around you."

"Actually, you were the only one who helped me keep it together."

"You sure about that? I thought maybe the reason you became friends with Richard was because he was a better father figure to you."

"Oh, Dad. No, that wasn't it at all. He just had a deep pain like I did. He understood that about me without me having to say a word about it."

"But you could share this stuff with him and not me."

"No, we never talked about it. Mostly we'd sit on his porch admiring the view and drinking coffee. He'd tell me about a book he read, and I'd explain the thought process behind a piece of furniture I was working on. That was it. But, Dad, you've always been the most important person in my life. Without you, I don't know that I would have made it. You accepted me where I was at. You never pushed. You always just loved me."

Sam grunted. "Well, I do love you. And right now, I really want to kill that guy Kyle. You sure they can put him away?"

"Yes. But if they can't, I've already said I can testify if they need me."

"If that happens, I'm coming with you."

"Good. I think I'd need you there."

He reached out and grabbed her hand, squeezing. "And I'm right here now. I won't let anything else happen to you."

"I appreciate the sentiment, but none of us can do that. And really, that's not even what I need. That's been my whole problem these last few years. I've been hiding from life, trying to make sure nothing else happened, but it still did. I've been living with my head in the sand thinking that the fear would protect me somehow."

"I wish I could have protected you better. If I hadn't let your mother — "

"Dad, don't. We can't keep looking back at the things we wish we could change. I'm ready to live again."

Sam put his arm around his daughter and pulled her tight, tears edging a path down his face. "I'm so proud of you."

"For what?"

"You've been through a lot, and you've come out the other side stronger than before. That says something about your character."

"I guess I could say the same about you."

"So what about Liam? What's going to happen to him?"

Emily bit her lip. She didn't want to say the inevitable out loud. "He'll go to prison, I guess."

"They should give him a medal is what they should do."

"But he's done stuff he shouldn't have, and he said he's ready to pay the price for that."

"I wouldn't normally encourage my daughter to visit a man in prison, but I'd make an exception here."

"He doesn't want me to." She dropped her head.

"What? Why not? What's wrong with him?"

"He wants me to move on with my life. He said he'd survive better in prison knowing that I had."

Sam let out a low whistle. "I'm liking this guy more and more. It's too bad things turned out this way. So you don't think you'll ever see him again?"

"No, I don't."

"Too bad. I saw the way you two looked at each other."

"I'm surprised at you."

"Why?"

"You're my dad and you want me in a relationship with a criminal?"

"Well, he's not just any criminal, is he? Anyone who saves my daughter — twice — and then tells her to live her life to the full deserves to have his past forgotten."

Sam pulled a blanket across their laps so they could enjoy the chilly morning a bit longer.

Emily snuggled up beside her dad and leaned her head on his shoulder. She sent up a silent thank-you to God for bringing her to this moment. Despite the loss of Liam, she was excited about the future for the first time in a long time.

Epilogue

ONE YEAR LATER …

Emily finished creating the ad for their latest Facebook blitz when her dad entered the office.

He leaned over her shoulder to see what she was doing. "I hope you don't expect me to keep that stuff going while you're away. You start talking about 'cost per click' and 'conversion rates' and my brain turns to mush."

"I already told you, I'll be keeping an eye on it. And I'm only away for a couple of days."

"But you'll be in the city."

"That's the magic of internet, Dad. I can mess with it even if I'm on the other side of the world."

"That's not such an impossible notion. Seeing your work featured all over the place, you never know what opportunity might open up. It's about time someone noticed how talented my little girl is."

"Mm. Okay, I'm going to head home and pack, but I'll see you before I leave."

"About that." Her dad cringed.

"Dad."

"I'm sorry. It's just that Patty went home sick — "

"Dad."

"It's only two hours till closing. Otherwise I would have called someone in. Besides, you don't leave until the morning, so you have plenty of time to pack."

"You know how much I hate waitressing."

"I know, but it won't be long. I just need you to jump in and serve section four, only until close."

Emily stood, gave her dad a dirty look, but then kissed him on the cheek and scooted around him. "This is the last time."

"Promise. And thank you."

She tied the standard maple-brown apron around her waist, shaking her head as she entered the dining room.

When she looked up, she frowned. It wasn't very busy. The other waitress who was working could have easily handled the load.

In fact, the section she was supposed to look after only had one customer. A guy with a baseball cap sat hunched over the table.

"Hey, Jen." She walked over to the other waitress. "Dad asked me to help serve, but do you mind looking after that guy over there? I can't imagine you'll get a rush anytime in the next two hours, and I've got to get packed."

"Uh …" Jen looked over at the guy, then back at Emily. "No, sorry. I've got stuff … to do." She turned quickly and hurried into the back.

Emily watched her go, her lip curled up in confusion. Jen was usually much more helpful. She sighed out her frustration and headed for her one occupied table.

"How are you today, sir? Are you ready to order, or do you need more time?"

The man scratched his forehead under his cap while he studied the menu. "Don't know. What do you recommend?"

"If I were you, I'd go with — " Her voice caught in her throat when he looked up at her. "Liam."

He took his cap off and stood.

Forgetting herself, Emily jumped forward and grabbed hold of him tightly, then realized what she had done and pulled back. Liam let go a little more slowly than she did.

Emily tucked her hair behind her ear. "Sorry, I'm just surprised to see you. I mean, I'm glad. I just … What are you doing here?"

His eyes lifted to look behind her. "You want to talk somewhere a little more private?"

She turned and found her dad and the other waitress watching from the side.

"Yes. Yes, I do."

Her dad waved at her as she passed by, blissfully uncaring at how uncomfortable it made her. She reached up and slapped his hand away.

She led Liam out the door. "There's a nice pergola over around the side."

When they walked up the steps to the undercover area, she had to resist the urge to grab hold of him again. She leaned instead against the balustrade with her hands tucked behind her.

He leaned on the handrail next to her. "You're looking well." His grin was as charming as she remembered it. It made her blush.

"Can I ask the obvious question of why you aren't in prison?"

"I was there for a little while, but it turns out I'm too valuable. Apparently, I was on an FBI list of some sort and when they found out about the knowledge I had, they used that and let me stay free. Well, sort of free. I've got someone I report to. I kind of work for them now. Getting information and cracking cases. You know, the usual."

"Wait, so you're telling me that because you came clean about everything you did, the FBI has hired you to work for them?"

"In a manner of speaking."

"How long has that been going on? Why didn't you come soon — sorry, I just — I thought you were in prison."

"Peter could have told you."

"I know. I didn't call him because I was afraid of what he'd say. It was safer to picture you in prison, believing you were safe and happy. I didn't want to know differently."

"I would have come sooner if I could have. Believe me. But I was under house arrest."

"You could have called?"

Liam heard the hurt in her voice and wanted more than anything to fix it. He turned away from her and walked across to the other side, stuffing his hands in his back pockets.

The maple trees that filled the acres behind the restaurant were filling with leaves again, just like last time he was there. Remnants of snow were piled in the permanently shadowed parts of the woods. "I wanted to."

"Then why didn't you?"

He turned. He hadn't been sure how he'd feel seeing her again after all this time, but nothing had changed for him. If anything, he wanted her more. "I needed to find myself first. I needed to find God again too. Without the distraction of another person. And I wanted to make sure you had that chance for yourself."

She nodded. "I heard about Kyle. I looked up his name online to see what his sentence was."

"Yeah, that actually hit me harder than I thought it would. I never expected him to kill himself. I think I still hoped he would come around."

"Yeah."

"But my sister got in touch not long after. She heard I'd turned myself in, and her husband, Brian, must have had a change of heart. So I've gotten to see my family again."

"I'm really happy to hear that."

"Looks like things have worked out well for you as well? I saw that feature they did on that renovation show."

"Did you see that?"

"I did. That's very nice work you're turning out."

"Yeah. I went from trying to drum up work to having to turn people down."

"So you're pretty busy, then?"

"Crazy busy."

"That's too bad."

"Why?"

"Well … you see … I have this house in town. Nice little house on top of the hill. It's got magnificent views, but not much furniture. And I thought maybe there was a local furniture maker who could help."

"Local furniture maker? Is that what you think of me?"

"No, not you. You're way out of my league." He moved closer. "I just thought you might be able to give me a recommendation."

She bit down on her grin. "I'm sorry, but I don't know of anyone who can help."

"That's too bad." He took another step closer. "I had hoped to settle in for a while, but I can't live there without anything to sit on or eat off."

"I think Walmart is having a sale on patio furniture." She couldn't hold back the smile this time.

"Patio furniture? Man, that is going to put a serious dampener on my love life. I can't invite a girl to my place if all I've got is patio furniture."

"I don't know. If you find the right girl, I don't think she'll care. Especially with that view you have up there."

"Oh, you know the view, do you?"

"I've been up there a time or two."

"Okay then, that settles it. Patio furniture it is. Now there's just one other thing."

"What's that?"

He took a last step forward so their toes were touching. "I know we haven't seen each other for a year, but I gotta be honest. I am dying to kiss you right now."

Emily ducked her head as she blushed. "That's, um — " She looked up and tipped her head sideways. "I, uh . . . "

He didn't waste any more time, just leaned forward and took the kiss before she could stumble across any more words. It was tentative at first, but they both fell into it quickly, wrapping desperate arms around each other. When they worked up the self-control to pull away, Emily still had her eyes closed.

He took a step back to get some air. He'd never been so overwhelmed by a person before. "Wow."

"Yeah."

"Not such a bad way to start things off." He reached for her and pulled her close.

"So we're starting something, are we?" she said, leaning into him.

"Okay, maybe continuing is a better word."

She breathed out a long, contented sigh. "No, you're right. This is a new beginning. For us both."

Enjoy the book?

Book reviews are the most powerful tool I have as an author to grow my readership. If I had the sway of a New York publisher, perhaps it would be easier to gain attention, but a simple reader review is way better than what any top publisher can offer…

Readers like yourself are what make the biggest difference to an author, and if you've enjoyed this book and wouldn't mind spending a few minutes leaving a review, it would help me out immensely.

Free Novella

One of the best things about being a writer is that I get to build relationships with my readers. And one of the best ways to do that is through a newsletter. I'm not a prolific emailer, but I will occasionally send out a newsletter with details on new releases, special offers, other projects I've been working on and anything else I have that might be of interest.

When you sign up, you'll get the prequel to the Shadow Alliance Series, free. This prequel tells the story of Peter and Jemi and how they met.

GET YOUR FREE EBOOK NOW

visit shawnacoleing.com

Also by Shawna Coleing

Shadow Alliance Series

SHADOW GAME - (Book 1 in the Shadow Alliance Series)

She must put her faith in a God she doesn't trust in order to save a man she can never have.

SHADOW BREAK - (Book 3 in the Shadow Alliance Series)

Solomon has never been afraid to die, until his latest assignment gives him something to live for.

Bristol Kelley Duology

A clean romantic suspense

SLEIGHT OF HAND

(Book 1 of 2 in Bristol Kelley)

Bristol ignores her conscience in order to work in the gray area of the law, but when a girl turns up murdered, she must enlist the help of her rival, Cole Sullivan, to stop a killer. But as the pair close in on the truth, Bristol has to face the consequences of her actions that may force her to do the unthinkable.

SMOKE AND MIRRORS

(Book 2 of 2 in Bristol Kelley)

Bristol thought she was free when she watched Silas walk

away in handcuffs. But when an important piece of evidence is thrown out on a technicality, she discovers Silas isn't the only one who wants to manipulate her.

Erin Hart Duology

A clean romantic suspense

OUT ON A LIMB - Book 1

A skilled thief who always gets what she wants, may lose it all when she risks everything to give her brother back the life that was stolen.

CUT TO THE CHASE - Book 2

She got all she thought she wanted...

It turned out to be more than she bargained for.

About the Author

Shawna Coleing is the author of the Shadow Alliance Series. You can find her on her website or feel free to contact her by email at:
shawnacoleing@pgturners.com

Otherwise you can connect with her here:

Any references to historical events, real people, or real places are used fictitiously. names, characters, and places are products of the author's imagination

First printing edition 2022